I won't tell you that Mary Tally's scheme was ethical. But when I looked at her I saw myself in different circumstances. I saw a woman with some brains in a country where women are valued for our bodies. I saw a black face where blackness is valued not at all. I could not judge her.

We had come from different places to arrive in this moment at the same place and with her story she was telling me the Secret. Letting me in on something, in case I didn't know it already, so it didn't jump up and bite me in my college-educated ass someday when I was unprepared. And she smiled a little when she saw I took her meaning, the way people smile at a small town scandal.

In the back of my mind, along with a fear of the dark I thought I'd outgrown, there was her smile and the words of Ralph Ellison's nightmare, "To whom it may concern: Keep this black boy running." And the sound of it was the sound of my own voice.

IN THE GAME

A VIRGINIA KELLY MYSTERY

IN THE GAME

NIKKI BAKER

The Naiad Press, Inc.
1991

Copyright © 1991 by Nikki Baker

Printed in the United States of America on acid-free paper
First Edition

Edited by Katherine V. Forrest
Cover design by Pat Tong and Bonnie Liss
    (Phoenix Graphics)
Typeset by Sandi Stancil

Library of Congress Cataloging-in-Publication Data

Baker, Nikki, 1962—
    In the game: A Virginia Kelly mystery / by Nikki Baker.
        p.   cm.
    ISBN 1-56280-004-3 : $8.95
    I. Title.
PS3552.A4327I5   1991
813'.54--dc20   91-22243
                                                         CIP

In memory of Michael Newman,
a good friend.

With thanks to Donna, Cynthia, Judith, Val
and especially Margaret.

About the Author

Nikki Baker was born in 1962. *In the Game* is her first novel. A second Virginia Kelly mystery, *The Lavender House Murder,* is scheduled to be published by Naiad Press in 1992. She is currently working on a third book in the series, *Long Goodbyes.*

I

Everything started to hit the fan just after my birthday in June. I didn't know it then, of course. I have no talent for clairvoyance. My gifts lie chiefly in a pleasant personality and wholesome good looks spread over a hard shell of cynicism like oak veneer is laid over plywood. I sell investment opinions on mutual funds for a living, telling people stories I make up. Real events often take me by surprise.

It surprised me, for instance, when Beverly called that night. First, we hadn't talked in months. Bev was riding the wave of a new romance courtesy of the personal ads. She had been dumped in February by some woman who had wanted an extended one night stand when Bev was looking for a relationship. But this new affair had put her back in the saddle. While it was good to see her happy again, I'll admit I resented that she didn't have a lot of time and energy for old friends.

Bev and I had gone to business school together, a vine-covered white people's institution whose black graduates numbered several hundred including those who were dead. We smiled at each other during graduation across an auditorium of pale faces, thinking we had it made, and I held my diploma up over my head afterwards like a key to the city while my father snapped our picture with a brand new automatic camera he'd bought for the occasion.

Bev and I had history, but I didn't like her new lover, Kelsey, much. Maybe because she was an object lesson in all the things I didn't like much in myself. I had spent the whole of my professional life, my formative years if you will, in the 1980s where you were what you owned. I won't say that I'd bought in completely, but it colors your thinking to grow up in financial services at a time when Donald Trump and Mike Milken are on everybody's pop culture A list.

To me, Kelsey was just more of the same old thing I was getting tired of. Her interests spanned only two topics: what she had just bought, and what she was going to buy. But she was a gregarious woman, happy with her things, and after a decade of relationships with women who were in social work and housing law Bev found her passion for

2

consumption novel. Whatever I thought of Kelsey, in the way of new romances, she and Bev only really had time for each other. So I made myself scarce.

The second reason I was surprised to hear from Bev was the time, nearly 11:30 pm, short notice for her to call about a drink. She was the kind of girl who'd call five days in advance to meet you for a cup of coffee at a diner down the street. But the bar was only a couple of easy blocks from my place. It was a beautiful night with a breeze off the lake and a moon like a cream pie. So I walked over to the bar to meet her.

I waited ten minutes for Bev to show up which was another surprise since I thought she'd called me from the bar. But that was okay with me. The Penguin, where she'd said to come, is a neighborhood place, homey and dark with that cheap paneling on the walls and hand-me-down equipment from all the other women's bars in this town that have opened and closed. The TV was turned on to some sporting event, but I don't understand sports so I was people-watching. The bar was crowded for a Wednesday, but no one in the place could really keep my attention. The woman behind the bar was holding court with four white girls in rolled-up blue jeans who all talked exactly alike. They all had identical black tank tops and skin only seconds away from puberty. I didn't know them; I didn't want to know them.

When the bartender finally got around to me, I ordered whatever was on draft and went back to checking out the people. I always order draft because it's cheaper. It bothers me to pay bar prices for a beer when I can drink a six-pack at home for the same money, even if the entertainment is better at a bar.

All the faces are familiar if you live in a town long enough, but I didn't know anyone well enough to speak. I put a dollar on the bar and settled down with my beer. A girl who had to have gotten in there with fake ID was working her way through the regulars. She was new and she was hopeful. She sat down next to me and waited for some conversation. I asked her how she was and then couldn't get rid of her. People say I have a kind face; it's a detriment in the city. They can smell generosity on you and I try to be hard but I can't pull it off. I'm the hard-bitten type that cries at Disney movies and opens her purse to the homeless. So I bought the girl a drink and she chewed my ear until I told her I was waiting for someone. Then she just stood up and walked away which was not what I intended. But it was just as well. My lover was out of town and I didn't need any under-aged complications in my life right now. Things were already sufficiently overwhelming. I was feeling trapped by my life.

After B-school I didn't know what to do. I was too tired to get a Ph.D and I owed more money in student loans than most families of four make in a year. So I got into financial services like everybody else. Now the only thing to differentiate me from the straight boys at my firm was race and sexual orientation. We were all marking time, waiting for the next bull market to make us so rich we didn't have to come into work anymore.

My father put himself through college working

the night shift at the Youngstown Steel Works and studying electrical engineering part-time. Sometimes he tells a story about one of the old-timers at the mill who said my dad wasn't a real steel worker. My father asked him why, looking down at himself, at the dirt on his pants and at his hands that were like sandpaper with the grit. The old man laughed and said it was because my father still had all of his fingers. He held out his own hands with three fingers and a stump and laughed some more. It was a joke to him in the way bitter facts of life are sometimes funny. But my dad didn't laugh. After that, he saved up his good union money and transferred to a college across the state and went full-time to school. When he graduated he went to work for the government, dejected because no one else would hire a black engineer in the 1950s.

My father always spoke his textbook English so that people cannot guess where he came from, but his skin color gave him away. He married my mother who is yellow and middle class, the third generation in her family to attend college, and he wore her like a disguise. They drummed their value system into me in stereo. For them it is about appearances. So I have pursued appearances as much as I can. I had no more choice as to how I would think or sound than if I had grown up disadvantaged in a housing project on the West Side or in the closet where B.F. Skinner put his kids, though I like to believe I am my own invention.

My father tried to give me the advantages he didn't have. He was embarrassed to have been named for a prize fighter, when the heavyweight title was the best that a black family could hope for their son. He was rigid in his vision of success and my queerness was a genetic wild card he could not have foreseen. If it were not for that, I think he would be proud of me.

As for myself, I thought a pay stub bigger than my bureaucrat father's monthly check would make me happy, but happiness has turned out to be more elusive than having all my fingers, an adjustable rate mortgage on the lake front and the Italian convertible I'm still paying on. Somehow it doesn't feel as good as it looked from a distance when I was living on my student loans in a south-side studio apartment and dreaming about corporate finance. Things were closing in on me and somewhere along the line I looked up to find I was a member of the bourgeoisie, but I didn't recall filling out a registration card. It was a startling discovery.

When Bev showed up she didn't look good. Bev was a black woman in the tradition of Miss Diana Ross, so that was uncharacteristic. She was committed to her appearance and she knew how to carry it off. Her mornings and evenings were consumed with a litany of personal grooming chores. Regimens to eradicate wrinkles, suppress sagging and maintain hair processed poker-straight so that it looked like a wig or the hair on a doll. Her lips were red like a 1940s movie star and she was tall and thin with legs that stretch forever. I envied and loved her beauty. Bev looked like she should have been my mother's child, while I am small, with pleasant, muted features and short wiry hair. I am a pretty girl whose looks neither stop traffic nor give offense.

The bar wasn't dark enough to hide the dark

circles under Bev's eyes. It was kind of a letdown to see her imperfections exposed, like seeing Times Square in the daytime, tired and gray without its neon trim. If glamour is art, Bev was looking like an unfinished creation in the Penguin that night. So much so that I was surprised she'd left the house. I had an idea of what the problem was, but I was going to wait for her to bring up the subject.

"How's it going?" I said.

"Not good." Bev stood in between my stool and an empty one, leaning over the bar and trying to make eye contact with the bartender. She shook her head in disgust. "Some people just can't be bothered to do their jobs."

I nodded. The bartender thought she was running a social club for regulars and her own particular buddies. She wore an oversized Madonna concert T-shirt the way some fat girls wear big clothes to make them look smaller.

"How are you?" said Bev. "It's been a while."

"Yes, it has. I thought you'd forgotten me." I was half kidding. Only half. It had hurt me that she hadn't called since the housewarming. I only had two good pals that I could depend on. Bev was one and Naomi was the other, but Naomi was starting to wear thin. The rest of my wide acquaintance was somewhat more off and on.

"Oh no, honey." Bev called everybody honey. It was just her way and I'd gotten to like it. "You know you're the best friend I have." She hugged me. When Bev hugged you, you knew she meant it. It was like a hug from your mother. It made me lonesome.

My parents lived out of state and I saw them

only twice a year at Christmas and Easter. It was less stressful that way. We talked about my job and my mother caught me up on who had gotten married; we avoided the subject of Em, my lover, by tacit agreement. My father would ask if I'd met any nice black men, and my grandparents who had lived long enough to have seen it all would find this cause for silent laughter. On the rare occasions when I came home in the summer telling myself I missed seeing grass and trees and really missing something else, we sat on the patio and drank, making conversation like people who are thrown together on a train. I would remember other summers, how we sat together when I came home from college, with my father marking off the courses I'd completed, and the chicken burning on the grill. I wanted to tell them on my visits how I had met a woman who I thought I loved, but remarked instead that the dog was getting old and had another drink.

"We don't have to talk all the time for you to know I'm always there for you," Bev said.

Bev was always there for me. She was right about that. She had carried me through our operations courses on her back and no doubt I had been heavy. Bev sold computers for Big Blue and somehow she'd developed an understanding of things like statistics and linear programming. For Bev, an MBA was definitely a terminal degree, a check mark by her name so that she wouldn't miss out because of a credential she didn't have, but worthy of as little effort as possible. She would let things slide for so long that I worried she might not pass, but she had a knack and Bev always made the grade. For me business school was a ticket into the game, a chance to play with the big boys and I took the course work seriously. Somehow at test time though she always beat me out.

"How's Em?" Bev asked as if she really wanted to know. Things weren't great. She told me how sorry she was and I shrugged. With me and Em things were good and then they were bad and then they were good again. Bev always took it more to heart than I did. Bev liked that I was married. She was the kind of woman who didn't mind that you had something she wanted; she was happy for you because she could imagine how much you were enjoying it.

"How's Kelsey?" I asked, trying to invoke that same kind of derivative emotion.

Bev kept waving at the bartender with no results. Finally she gave up and sat down on the stool next to mine. She laid down her purse and traced the grooves in the bar with her red fingernails and sighed. "I don't know what's going on with Kelsey."

I watched her fingers. They were long and thin. Usually her nails were symmetrical and perfect. Bev had a regular appointment with the manicurist that she was loath to miss. Tonight, one nail was badly chipped. It might have spoiled the tableau for some people but for me Bev was still one of the small aesthetic miracles of the world even with the bags under her eyes and her nails in need of a new paint job. I will confess to you that Bev Johnson was my secret weakness, the friend we all have whom we have imprudently fallen for and value too highly to fuck. She was the good jewelry I was afraid to wear out in public, but still I liked to look at her.

9

"I think Kelsey's seeing someone else," she said.

"I doubt that," I lied. "Why do you think so?"

Bev sighed again. "I should have picked someplace with tables."

"This is fine," I said. "Don't worry."

The bartender finally sauntered over and took our orders like it was a big favor. When the drinks came, I stiffed her on the tip. We got up and moved to one of the little ledges along the wall. They were less comfortable but more private. Bev was having white wine. I had another beer. My confidence in the wine selection at a place like this was slim.

Truth be told, I was surprised again that Bev had suggested the Penguin. The Bar Madrid or Gloria's Place, the upscale girls' bars, were more her style unless she wanted to be sure that nobody who mattered caught her act looking like she did. Or maybe she thought I wouldn't drag myself all the way to Madrid or Gloria's at 11:30 pm on a Wednesday. She was probably right on that count. Both those places were in Uptown, a lousy neighborhood where they could afford to rent a lot of space. I didn't like to go there by myself on an off-night when there weren't a lot of people around.

Of course, there had been a scandal about a year before at Gloria's over requiring more IDs for blacks and latinas than for white girls. They had a sign by the door that gave management the right to ask for up to five IDs to get in. On Friday and Saturday nights some women of color were complaining that management asked them to show more ID than some white girls from the suburbs who were in front of them in line. Other women complained that one of the owners who had always seemed all right to me dressed up in black-face and wore fruit on her head for an Island Night promotion. There was a loose kind of boycott for a while and a lot of people wrote letters to the gay papers. The white owners felt maligned. The patrons of color felt discriminated against. By way of apology, Gloria's instituted Wednesdays for women of color. There was no cover during the week and the DJ played music you could dance to. On Fridays and Saturdays, however, Gloria's still played music designed to drive anyone with an ounce of natural rhythm away.

I don't know how much of all this was true; I had never been asked for more than one ID at Gloria's, but I stopped going there on principle. Maybe Bev had too. In my mind, it came down to color, class and money. Almost everything does. If you have enough money and you're middle class, it's okay to be black or latina. It's not okay to be a working-class woman of color in an upscale, white, northside bar, but if you're white nobody cares what your class is as long as there is money enough in your pocket for the five-dollar cover.

The only thing that didn't take me by surprise that night was the news about Kelsey. Naomi Wolf and I had had a handle on that for some time, since the housewarming party Bev and Kelsey had given in May.

A few weeks before on a Saturday night, I was standing in their yard eating little meatballs and swilling the free beer. Naomi was making a meal of gin and cigarettes and bending my ear about her prospects in the District Attorney's office. From what I gathered they were pretty good. But that figured. Naomi was the daughter of a Democratic machine patrician, an old powerful man with hair growing out of his ears.

She held her thumb and index finger just barely apart and waved them in my face. "Ginny, I'm this close to a judicial appointment," she said, drunk and elated. "I can almost taste it." Naomi was a long-range planner. To her "this close" meant years.

"Yeah?" My lover Emily was cornered by some woman in a batik crop top who looked like she made Chicago Health Club commercials for a living, and I couldn't get too interested in Naomi's career development.

"Yeah," said Naomi. "People are going to say I didn't earn it, but fuck 'em. I earned it." Sometimes Naomi cracked me up.

"Hey," she said, "are you listening to me?"

"Sure," I said. "You know, maybe I should lose a little weight." I had put on some pounds since I started living with Em. Not a lot, but I had noticed. Em had noticed.

"You look great," Naomi said absently. Naomi could talk to you and watch the door at the same time without you minding much. It's her nature, always looking for a better opportunity. I was used to it.

"You think?" I said.

"Sure." Naomi popped the top on another beer and put it in my hand. "You look great." She was watching Em and Ms. International Abdominal Muscles too, but I couldn't tell who interested her most. "Don't let it get you down." She patted me on the head and wandered off towards Em's new friend.

Naomi and I went back a long way. She was older by about seven years and didn't hesitate to

12

remind me of it and that gave me a pain. Otherwise, Naomi was okay. As we got older, it seemed to me that the age gap was narrowing, but she still looked on my relationships as short-term propositions owing to my immaturity. Naomi slept with a gold coast matron she'd met in the locker room of her health club, an arrangement she characterized as a commitment.

Naomi Wolf was a world-class party circulator. Given twenty minutes she could meet everyone of interest in a convention hall. Between her glad-handing and her political connections, it was no wonder someone was going to make her a judge someday before senility set in. I hadn't even finished my beer by the time she got back around to me. Like a bloodhound, Naomi had found whatever dirt there was to find at this party and her eyes fairly glowed with fresh intrigue — that or gin. She hooked her arm in mine and led me inside to Bev's bathroom for some privacy.

The building Kelsey owned was a rehabbed two-flat in a gentrified neighborhood for which she had paid handsomely. Almost everything but the brick shell had been gutted and rebuilt. Developers were doing that all over the city. They would pick up some structure that needed body work for a song and then remake it into an up-scale, live-in investment for yuppies — a brand new suburban interior in the middle of town. With commuting time at a premium, financial services was turning this into a white-collar city, when a few years ago the ticket for a young professional was a place in the suburbs. Now people were willing to pay for the privilege of living in what used to be a slum, sure that the real estate boom would never end and that some other patsy waiting down the line would take them out at a profit.

Kelsey's place was very nice. It had two completely separate apartments, with separate entrances connected by the stairs of the back porches, in the typical style of the Chicago brick two-flat. Bev rented the bottom flat from Kelsey for appearances, but they lived in both flats. The rent, Bev told me, was to help out, which was only fair, and the lease was for appearances and the tax man.

Bev's bathroom was a Euro-style affair with a bidet and a wall-hung toilet. The floor was black marble and the walls were stark white. Contrast was very in this year but it was making me a little dizzy. I sat down on the toilet. Naomi closed the door — mostly for effect. Naomi is like that.

"All right, Naomi," I said. "What's going on?" My head was starting to hurt.

Naomi sat herself on the side of the Jaccuzzi tub. She reached across to the toilet and squeezed my knee with delight. "Kelsey's got another woman on the side."

I let my mouth hang open stupidly. "Does Bev know?"

"Of course not," she said. "That's what makes it so good."

"Right," I said, unconvinced. I don't covet bad news the way Naomi does. "But how do you know?"

Naomi rolled her eyes and made a smacking sound with her tongue on the back of her teeth. "I'm getting to that." She waved away my interruption with both hands. "Don't rush me, okay? I was talking to Kelsey's closing lawyer while you were drinking. She told me Kelsey bought this place because her lover was moving from Boston to live with her and they needed more room."

"I don't get it," I said. "Bev's not from Boston."

Naomi rolled her eyes some more. "That's exactly the point." She pinched my knee again, much harder, and I complained.

"Oh shut up." Naomi continued. "Anyway, the lawyer asked me if Beverly was from Boston. Apparently she's asked Beverly too. Don't you love it?"

"Not a lot, Naomi," I said. "Did this lawyer say anything to Bev?" The last thing I wanted was for Bev to get hurt again.

"I told you she asked her if she was from Boston." Naomi tapped some ash from her cigarette into the sink. I hoped she would clean it up, but I doubted it.

"No," I said. "About the lover."

Naomi shook her head. "No. Frankly, I don't think she figured it out until I suggested that maybe Kelsey had two girlfriends and she was just talking to the wrong one. When I told her Beverly's idea of the east coast was Saggatuck, Michigan, she clammed up and faded away." Naomi shrugged. "No loss. The girl had the charm of a Sherman tank."

"Very nice, Naomi," I said. "So what are we going to do?" Though at the moment I wasn't sure I could do much of anything. I was beginning to regret the amount of beer I'd consumed and was tasting meatballs I hadn't seen for more than an hour. The last thing I needed was to apprise a good friend of her lover's infidelities — not at their housewarming at least. And I reassured myself that I had not liked Kelsey from the beginning — out of some psychic foreshadowing rather than my jealousy at being displaced as number one in Bev's priorities. It was the bitter satisfaction that comes from having expected things to turn out badly and having been proved right.

"We could sit back and watch the fireworks when Beverly finds out she's been hosed," Naomi suggested.

I didn't like that idea. I was closest to Bev and it would be me who had to tell her anyway. I wanted to delay that episode. The longer, the better. I hoped this was just a strange misunderstanding.

"Why don't we do some detective work?" I said. "I wouldn't want to tell that to Bev if it wasn't true."

Naomi agreed to chat up the lawyer some more and report back. It seemed the most sensible of two bad alternatives.

It had always pained and amazed me that a woman as beautiful as Bev was dumped so often. Between girlfriends, Bev could sit up in the bars all night with not even a free drink or a phone number to show for it. White girls who looked like they hadn't washed their hair in months would get picked up in fifteen minutes. I am inclined to chalk it up to good old-fashioned American racism. Not a problem of policy, but one of preference giving rise to the sad reality that black women have to be about ten times better looking than your average white dyke in flannel to get noticed at a majority watering hole. And in our own places, where we can find each other expecting nothing short of perfect understanding, there is the serial disappointment of a reflection that is both different and the same. It is staggering how deeply we must know and love ourselves as black women to kiss the mirror with open eyes.

These generic difficulties were complicated for Bev because she suffered badly from wanting to be married, really married — not just on cold nights when she was lonely and there were no new releases at the video store. That scares the girls away unless you already are married in which case they flock to you in droves. This is why when I first became involved with Em, women I didn't know suddenly struck up conversations with me in bars. The more unavailable you are, the more attractive.

So many things are more desirable when they belong to other people. This universal truth applies to much more than dating. It is why to borrow money, you must first prove you don't really need it, and it's the reason you should never look for a job unless you already have one. This fact of human nature is the source of such truisms as "all the good ones are taken," and the reason that love of epic proportions always seems to contain a healthy dose of adultery. The state of the world in tandem with the need for some equal opportunity cruising put a real crimp in Bev's social life until she answered Kelsey's personal ad in a gay rag.

Within a week, they were hot and heavy. Within a month, I was eating Swedish meatballs and getting sick at their housewarming. As big a bore as I thought she was, Kelsey was certainly the package that Bev was waiting for, an educated professional girl ready to settle down and able to pay for two vacations a year: one ski, one sun. I was happy for

Bev. To Bev, the money and the status mattered. Though as near as I could tell she did all right for herself. She had expensive tastes and an appetite for new clothing, and mostly she spent her bonuses before they were earned in lots of ways she couldn't remember afterwards. Bev had been waiting for someone who could keep up with her economically.

It seemed to me that that line of thinking was getting less unusual. Dykes are always a day late and a dollar short on societal trends. A decade ago lesbians were shopping at second-hand stores and shouting "Take back the night" while the rest of America decided it was going to live in the material world. Now all those thirtysomething-style Yuppies were looking for something more than an increase in their credit limits, but dykes had lately discovered consumption. Educated, professional lesbians had become a brand of trade to be served up in the personal ads.

Don't misunderstand me. I'm all for upward mobility and I like personal ads, especially the men's. They have a certain *joie de vivre* that lesbians, while they are trying, have never quite mastered. The men's personals are straightforward like the want ads or the classifieds: Top man wants bottom for hot, safe nights. No drugs, no femmes need apply.

The womens' ads are more subtle and confused. Women are still learning how to ask for what they want. I started reading the womens' ads regularly when Em announced we should both get into therapy to deal with her neuroses. Em needed her space, she said, but when I backed away she didn't need that much. We were at that difficult three-year point in our relationship where the sex stops and you fight about it.

"You want to sleep with that Naomi," said Em. "You want to sleep with that checker at the Jewel, the cute, black one and the Oriental woman at the cleaners. I've seen how you look at her."

"I only want to be with you," I promised her, though I wasn't completely sure at times that this was true, and whined that there was no passion in our relationship anymore. Em contended that I wanted my life to be like an X-rated movie, but when I first met her she wanted to do it in the street and I wondered where that had gone. There was love. We had grown comfortable and used to each other, but now Em's passion was exhibited mostly in her jealousy.

There were good days too when she would wrap her whole body around me and whisper in my ear that I was beautiful and if we hurried, we could have one orgasm each before the alarm went off. Em had her old energy then, working against the clock to show me how much I still resembled the woman I was three years ago when sleep seemed unimportant to her. Em wanted me on her terms. I wanted her, but I wanted a romance that would subordinate all other feelings like romance does when it is new. In the face of our differences racial and otherwise, I wanted a woman who could finish my sentences, who knew the rules to bid whist.

On the bad days, it was a rock and a hard place. On the bad days, I read the personal ads in the gay papers in detail as if I would be tested on the contents. There are three varieties: kinky, expensive or dull. The dull ads come in two colors: black/latina and white/latina lending credence to the thought that now is the optimal time to be a latina lesbian.

Example 1: Kinky

GWF, 28 secure medical professional in NW suburbs. I enjoy quiet intense times with attractive androgynous women rather than the maddening crowd. Like traveling, camping, music, cats and leather. If you are open-minded, emotionally stable, not into heavy drinking/drugs and willing to explore your sexual limits — with trust, please write.

Example 2: Expensive

GF. 40 femme lesbian looking for fun and excitement. Would you like to travel or go out on the town for an evening but hate to go alone? I have a zest for living and enjoy many things. Alas I have no money. You pay all expenses and let's have fun. No strings! Excellent references.

Example 3: Dull

a. GWF, professional seeks feminine GW/GHF for possible relationship.

b. GBF, educated professional seeks feminine GB/GHF for possible relationship.

It comes down to an enduring question. Which would you choose: order and peace, or passion and craziness? I thought I wanted passion, but not enough to pursue it. I wanted it to come looking for me and then roll past like the frames of a film leaving me just as I was before it started.

Aside from the personal ads which did me no good, I read the gay papers from cover to cover each week when they came out. The existence of a gay press generates a reassuring sense of community for an invisible minority. Reading a gay paper is like pinching yourself and finding you are really there. Besides, the papers are free and I never have to wonder how adversely they're going to impact my weekly budget. I suppose, too, I read them out of a sense of nostalgia having met my lover, Emily, in the business classifieds.

Three years ago I called my father to ask for a loan. He suggested I needed a financial planner since he couldn't figure out how I could possibly be having a tight month on my salary. I told him it was expensive to live in the city, but he wasn't buying it. He said I needed either a financial planner or drug rehab, wished me luck and hung up. So, I hired an accountant from the gay and lesbian business guide, Emily Karnowski.

Em was tall and blonde and not too possessive; she relegated most of her butch behaviors to the bedroom. I liked that. I liked her too, right away. She reminded me oddly of my father with her boat-people work ethic and her second-generation American need to be somebody.

Over the years, I'd gotten used to the derision that comes to black people with white spouses. I received the quiet intimations of self-hate the same way I took the speculation by my mother that my lifestyle was an illness that I ought to have treated. Whatever else she was, Em was proud that she had been the first generation in her family to go to college and I liked that she understood the difference between right and privilege more than I cared that she'd grown up in a neighborhood where no one would sell me a house. We had grown up in the same way, if separately, with parents who wanted for us a little more than what they had. Who had sacrificed for their families and counted progress by the accomplishments of the next generation rather than the possessions of their own. We shared a sameness of aspiration that was something I felt that I could hold onto when I was looking for things to anchor my own values.

On top of that, her rates were reasonable and she was handy too which was a package I couldn't resist, my mother having raised me to know a bargain. Em painted my condo and fixed my toilet within a week of our first appointment. In two months, I was solvent. In six months she had moved in and was working out of my extra bedroom with her computer and her file drawers. Now, Dad asked politely over the phone how my roommate and I were getting on and wished he had just sent me the money when I asked.

Em took care of my bills gratis, though she insisted that she was being paid — in "trade." Em was an exceptional accountant, solid and humorless, paying half my mortgage and parcelling out a tiny allowance each week from my accounts. In the three years we'd lived together, she'd saved me big bucks not including my retirement fund contributions. We had a joke that I couldn't afford to leave her. It was one dollar each way to work on the bus, another ten dollars per week for the *Trib* and the *Journal* and I still had to each lunch every day. The way Em had it set up I couldn't leave her, since on my allowance I couldn't afford to date. I wasn't even sure I wanted to. But there was no telling Em that when she walked in on Naomi and me in the bathroom and announced that it was time to go home.

Naomi laughed. There had never been any love lost between the two of them. Em maintained that Naomi was spoiled and a terrible influence, appealing to my tendency to drink too much and flirt with women I met in bars. Naomi contended that Em was stiff and joyless. They were both right.

Emily pulled me by the arm and I found that I was standing. Em is a big girl. She did her best to ignore Naomi.

"You look like shit, Virginia Kelly," she said to me. She was right. I felt like shit. "I've asked you not to drink so much."

"Great party, huh," said Naomi.

Em made a grunt in Naomi's direction and walked out, presumably towards my car, so I followed her.

Naomi waved. "I've asked you not to drink so much," she called after me. I could still hear her laughing from the hall.

We ran into Kelsey and Bev on the patio. Em didn't want to stop to speak, but Kelsey was no small girl and it was hard to get around her.

Em kissed Bev on the cheek and said: "See you later." Em liked Bev as much as I did. Sometimes I was jealous and I didn't even know of whom.

"Where are you going so fast, honeybunch?" said Bev. There was still a lot of food and they hadn't put the dessert out yet.

Kelsey hugged us both in her athletic way, slapping our backs men's club style. "Stick around, girls. I haven't seen you two all night." Kelsey was shouting to hear herself over the party music, but I had started to sober up and my head was killing me.

"It's a great party," said Em, "but Ginny's feeling sick."

Kelsey peered at me through her schoolboy glasses and laughed. It was like a single blast from some big wind instrument, short and monotonic. "We should have cut you off hours ago, woman," she pronounced. "You look green."

"I feel green," I said and Kelsey roared. I kissed Bev, and Em said goodnight again.

Em didn't want to hear about Kelsey's extra girlfriend or my proposed investigation. The ride home was very cool. With the Cubs playing on TV Sunday, Em wasn't lonely enough to make up and barely spoke to me all that day. Em can hold a grudge. Things didn't begin to thaw until Monday morning, but sometimes making up is worth the fight.

I had a meeting first thing Monday. When I got out at 11:30 am, there was a pile of messages on my chair. My secretary was in the habit of putting them there so they wouldn't get lost in the clutter on my desk. One from Naomi on the top of the pile said "Re: Lunch" so I looked at my watch and put the message on the bottom. I was still holding my own grudge for this weekend's domestic strife. By the time I'd cleared my desk and returned my other calls it was 1:30 pm. Nearly everybody I had tried to reach was at lunch, of course, but I had successfully put the ball back in their courts.

This is the beauty of phone tag. If you time your return calls correctly, you never need actually talk to anyone. If you never actually talk to clients, they can never request the impossible — extra services like the augury, clairvoyance and witchcraft the marketing department has promised that you would love to provide to them. But if you always return their calls how can they complain you are unresponsive? After a while, time will answer their questions. They will buy and hold their solid investments which is what you would have advised anyway; and in the long-term they will make some money. In the short term, they will never have unpleasant memories of how you personally told them to buy some trendy stock because it had hit bottom only to have it resume free fall within the week.

I liked to make my recommendations in writing in our monthly releases with the appropriate caveats. It was safer. An old timer had told me once that investment advice was a no-win game; people expect it when you're right and when you're wrong, you're incompetent. My ability to win at phone tag was key to my mental health and job security at good old Whytebread and Greese.

My secretary, Starr, brought in four other messages from Naomi who had clearly asked her to convey a sense of urgency. But all the messages were regarding lunch. God knows what Starr had managed to misunderstand about the nature of our relationship.

I promised Starr I would call Naomi which I did at about 2:00 pm hoping she had given up and gone on to lunch already. Naomi was still hanging around, but she wasn't happy about it.

"It's about time," she said.

"Yeah?" I said. "Well maybe you're not on my 'A'

list right now." I wasn't pissed anymore, but I thought she deserved a little guilt trip.

Of course Naomi wasn't buying it. She assured me that she didn't experience guilt anymore and even offered to give me the name of the therapist responsible. My father had called last week and I was considering taking her offer. "Meet me at Wendy's on Dearborn and Madison," she said. "And by the way, Ginny, cut the crap." Then she hung up.

I got my jacket and on the way out passed Starr fixing her platinum and brown hair in a little mirror at her desk. I told her I'd be back in an hour. Maybe Naomi would buy lunch.

Of course, Naomi wasn't buying lunch. She wasn't even eating lunch. She was consuming Diet Coke and nicotine. I ordered a Wendy's double and bought her another Coke. At least her mood had improved in the five minutes it had taken her to walk over from Daley Plaza. Under her arm she had an expandable cardboard folder, the kind with a flap and a little string to tie it closed. She was smiling from ear to ear. I sat down and she opened the folder and slid a green postcard over to my side of the table.

"Do you know what this is?" Naomi asked me.

I didn't.

"Investigative materials," Naomi announced. The postcard was a change of address form typed out with Kelsey's name and current address. It indicated Kelsey would like her mail sent to a post office box from now on.

Naomi pulled a key out of her enormous power purse and put it down on top of the postcard. She didn't say anything. My double burger was getting cold. "So we steal Kelsey's mail," I said. "I don't get it."

Naomi didn't answer. She had her nose in her bag digging for more cigarettes. Eventually she found a pack of Marlboro Lights and fired one up. "If you really wanted to find out whether Kelsey had another girlfriend this is how you'd do it."

She leaned back in her chair and blew a stream of smoke out over her head. "Drop the postcard in the mail and Kelsey won't figure out that she's not getting her mail for at least one billing cycle — maybe longer. By that time you'd have all her bills and anything else you need to know if the lawyer at the party was right." Then she looked at me as if to say, "I don't know how you stay employed as stupid as you are."

Okay. The plan had charm. "What if you get caught," I asked. I had no idea what the inside of Dwight Women's Prison looked like and wanted to keep it that way.

Naomi laughed, blowing smoke out everywhere. "Nobody but you and American Express care about Kelsey's mail. But you won't get caught. The post office box is in Kelsey's name," she said. "Don't you love it." Naomi tapped her cigarette on the little glass ashtray on the table and crossed her arms.

I wasn't sure that "love" was exactly the right word, but I had an itch. It was the itch that made Eve take the first apple, the reason Pandora had to open the box.

I looked at my watch. I had another meeting in ten minutes. "All right, what's a little mail tampering between friends?" I put the green postcard in my purse then collected the paper from my lunch and put it on the tray to throw out.

Naomi shook her head, giggling. "No. No. No. No. No. I was just joking." She took hold of my arm as I got up. "Sometimes I don't believe you, Ginny."

I pointed out that it didn't sound like she was joking a minute ago. "It sounded more like recruiting a minute ago," I said. "So why don't you just stop being coy."

That set her off. Naomi was indignant. "I wasn't being coy. You know, mail tampering is a federal offense. That's nothing to be coy about. You can't just steal someone's mail," she reminded me as if she were carrying down the Tablets with the word of God, all filled with Old Testament piss and fury.

I picked up the key and tossed it back at her. "It was your idea," I said. "What's this?"

"That's my mailbox key, you dope." Naomi was pissed.

I didn't care. She'd pissed me off lots of times. "Then what's the point?" I said.

"There is no point. It was a joke." Naomi was shouting. "Just because I know how to break the law doesn't mean I would seriously do it." Naomi believed that the louder she talked the righter she was, but the litigator's tactic didn't work on me. I knew her too well; I knew her when she was still fine-tuning her rhetoric.

"You're shouting, Naomi," I said.

She smoothed the top of her hair and took a deep breath. "That's because this is important and I'm trying to get your attention."

I assured her that she had it.

"I just hope, Ginny, that you're not considering a stunt like that for real," Naomi said.

"No," I lied. "Not a chance."

Naomi seemed genuinely relieved, and I left with the typed postcard still in my purse. When I looked back at her from the street she was smoking and smiling like she'd just told herself a good one.

II

On my budget, Em had explained, it was too expensive to drive my car to work and pay for parking, a luxury in which I indulged before she took over my finances. I was riding public transportation which I promise you is a slice of life.

Chicago has one of the best public transportation systems in the world. Partially built in the 1890s as a technological spectacle for the Columbian Exposition, it efficiently links neighborhoods of people who hate each other to the Loop, downtown Chicago, the center of business. The El is fast. It can get you from as far as O'Hare Airport outside of the city to Marshall Field's main department store on State Street in a half an hour which is an impossibility by car if you take the Kennedy Expressway anytime other than five o'clock in the morning. But at rush hour it was a bit like being packed in a sardine can, with people's arms and elbows jammed into your back. Non-rush hour it was filled with a cross-section of the kind of people who made me nervous: young aimless men, teenagers in packs and homeless people.

Instead, I took the express bus down LaSalle Street in the financial district, past traffic court, through Old Town and on up the Lakefront. Even on the express, it takes forty-five minutes to go thirty blocks. The bus is slow, and going north there are a lot of stops and always a few black faces.

In Chicago, as late as the 1960s, the realtor's code of ethics forbade selling a house in a white neighborhood to a black family, though sometimes it happened by mistake when black families, so light-skinned that they could pass for white, did not explain that they were not. Riots resulted in places with names like the Airport Homes, Trumbull Park, and Cicero, a white ethnic suburb which has not changed much in forty years. The riots saw that mistakes were quickly corrected.

In Chicago, race hate and prejudice cross barriers of class and money. Consequently, middle-class neighborhoods as well as slums and housing projects are still segregated for the most part. People are territorial even in their poverty. It is why, in Chicago, you can get the most authentic ethnic food and the stoniest looks at the same time. Why the

South Side is the largest contiguous community of black people on the North American continent. Why the west-side neighborhoods that created the likes of Saul Bellow and William Paley changed color overnight and panic-peddling real estate agents made fast-money fortunes by buying houses cheap from Jewish families and selling dear to black ones. Why in exclusive suburbs north of the city, rich WASP's pull their children out of history classes in protest because they contend that the Holocaust was fiction.

There are few truly integrated neighborhoods, and questions of money, religion and class only serve to complicate things. On the South Side where I could live quietly as a lesbian because black people will look the other way for their own, I could not live with Em. So we live together on the Lakefront where I am lonely for clean-scrubbed, hard-working brown faces that would have a smile and a word for me on the bus. Going north, there are mostly the pale, closed expressions of people who moved a little closer to the window when I took a seat beside them. The old ladies on the bus clutched their bags a little tighter when a black man beside me made his way down the aisle. When I met his eyes, in that instant we communicated volumes, every page that will ever be written as he opened his *Wall Street Journal* knowing why I was happy to let the shoulders of our suit jackets brush each other in our seats. I stared ahead and out the window listening to the conversation of two men behind me and played the game of trying to guess what they looked like. One was, I guessed, a gay white man with pattern baldness. He had a quiet voice and had just bought a 1920s club chair from an antique store in my neighborhood. Both men gushed as he described the chair which had the original upholstery. They got off the bus at Belmont with a million other people and I was disappointed, unsure of who they were in the crowd. Another unsolved mystery.

I've been a hopeless mystery buff since I was a kid. I like mysteries where a regular guy is the hero like Cary Grant in *North by Northwest,* Jimmy Stewart in *Rear Window,* and a million different books and movies they show late at night on local UHF channels. I can always guess who did it before the bumbling hero and I say to myself: "I could do that." Investment is a little like a detective novel; there are clues, bodies are buried and your job is to find them for your clients. That's why I couldn't throw the green change-of-address card away when I got back to my office. The more I thought about Naomi's plan, the more I thought it would work. I would do a favor for Bev and no one would catch me. People ask the question: Is there sound if a tree falls in the forest and no one hears it? It seemed to me the answer was no.

III

The post office box where I sent Kelsey's mail was downtown on Adams Street, the big main one across from the Marquette Building. I went there at lunch once a week for three weeks to get the mail. Then, I would take it out to read it in the sun on First National Plaza over my box lunch. On a nice day in the summer, the Plaza is wall-to-wall people spread out with their sandwiches and their papers like a day at a concrete beach. Even so, it had a kind of privacy, the anonymity that is found in crowds.

I went on Fridays and paid some different homeless person to go in and bring the mail out to me. I always picked women. It seemed that they were more likely to spend the money on food. My favorite one was a black woman with two winter coats and a blanket in the middle of the summer, who slept in front of the Palmer House Hotel on the Monroe Street side. Every day the doormen would chase her off their sidewalk and she would curse them saying she had just as much right as everybody else. Every night she would come back and sleep just down the street from the entrance. There was a dark spot close to the building where she had peed for spite and a faint smell of urine even though they washed the sidewalk down regularly. I hired her twice. When I gave her the money, she took it like it was due her. She didn't say thank you like I was doing her a favor and I liked that; we are too apologetic as a race.

In the meantime, I really started to get into the cloak and dagger stuff, patting myself on the back for my cleverness. I had a little fantasy of a new career with the CIA if I could scheme how to get past the sexual orientation questions on the lie detector test. I worried that Kelsey was missing her mail, but I didn't want to stop. I liked the rush that came as the week drew closer to Friday. I slept less and less at night until on Thursday nights, I barely slept at all.

I was lucky. By the third week, I had the phone

bill, a bank statement and some incriminating correspondence. It was pure voyeurism, looking into someone's life without her knowing. It was a kick, omnipotence, like watching a movie, armchair thrills, the kind you can walk away from.

Em always says that in her business, financial planning, a bank statement is worth a thousand words. When she's feeling romantic she makes me sit in her lap with her arms around my waist and whispers that with us it was fate the first time she saw my financials because she knew I really needed her. When I saw Kelsey's financials I knew she really needed Bev.

A trip back through the land of canceled checks said that Bev was kicking in about half of what Kelsey was paying to Horizon Federal Savings and Loan. Utilities were not included. The deposit slips said Kelsey didn't make nearly as much money as I would have guessed from her lifestyle and she was seriously strung-out on consumer credit. The whirlwind courtship was starting to make sense to me.

Have an appetite for upscale living, but limited means? Find some woman to subsidize you. I had some pangs of guilt around this concept but quickly rationalized that I had incurred my mortgage debt some years before I found Em to help me pay it. And she did get to write off her rent as a home office deduction. It struck me as sad and funny that Bev, who was so sure she was getting economic parity, had been married for her cash flow.

The phone bills were astronomical. Kelsey called Boston all the time. I used the name and address service to find out who went with what numbers.

She called the Boston girl from home on nights when I remembered Bev was out of town on business. My guess was Kelsey called her more often than that, but from her office, and I was just lucky that Bev had been gone so much that month on sales calls and trade shows.

Then there was the correspondence. The Boston girlfriend sent cards the way some people send love letters. Sometimes she would send two a week. They were the kind of cards you can buy at gay specialty shops. One had a drawing of a tan woman with straight black hair and big mirror sunglasses. Another woman's butt, in a skirt so tight it dipped in at her legs and you could see her cheeks through the fabric, was drawn reflected in the mirrors. The written contents were pretty much in harmony with the art work. Kelsey's pen pal drew meticulous circles over her i's for dots. In a postscript she asked how Kelsey's new tenant was working out. I wondered what Kelsey wrote back.

Her girl was very young, and I imagined very hot, probably with a butt that looked good in a tight skirt. I was ready to bet dollars to donuts she was probably white, but that was my baggage. The letters were sophomore pornography.

Naomi nearly lost her mind when I showed them to her.

"You dumbshit," she said, and I could tell she meant it. "Do you want to go to jail? Do you want me to go to jail for knowing about this?"

I hadn't planned to tell Naomi what I'd done, but the letters were too disturbing not to share the misery. They were, of course, just the kind of thing Naomi likes.

"Will you stop calling me names, Naomi," I complained. "Relax. You're the one who said I couldn't get caught this way."

Naomi smacked herself on the forehead and groaned. "I didn't know for sure, you idiot. Goddamn," she said. "I hope I'm as smart as you think I am."

I wasn't worried. Naomi's pretty smart, but the whole thing started to make me a little sick after a while on account of Bev. Now that I knew for sure, I would have to tell her.

From the phone bill and utilities, nothing in the upstairs apartment was in Bev's name. It was a straight tenant arrangement with Bev installed for appearances in the basement apartment.

That made sense. According to Bev, Kelsey was a complete closet case who insisted on separate apartments and made Bev sign a lease agreement to make it kosher. Bev had complained to me when she moved in that she didn't understand why they needed separate spaces when they were so much in love. Later Bev said that Kelsey was moody and the nights she spent in the upstairs apartment were becoming less frequent.

I didn't know if the idea of another woman had crossed Bev's mind, but it seemed to me that Kelsey was less of a closet case than a pragmatic girl with plans for her future. She was thinking maybe Bev would stay on as a tenant when her new woman moved in upstairs. Then her problems would be solved. She'd have her lover upstairs and a lesbian tenant with a good payment history already moved in downstairs. From the correspondence, she hadn't even told the Boston girlfriend, whose name was Mary, about Bev. I have no idea how she planned to arrange the breakup. But there are lots of ways to do that.

Once Naomi told me she had tired of a lover and pretended to lose interest in sex. After a while the woman left her in disgust. But Naomi's ex-girlfriend always had a condescending hug for her whenever they met again, sure that it was she and not Naomi who had decided their affair was over. The thought of that kind of game played on Bev made me almost sorry for the minor league dirt I'd done to my own unwanted lovers.

Naomi was all for telling Bev the story she'd heard from the lawyer at the party and watching the fireworks, but omitting the part about the mail. She argued we'd be doing Bev a favor. Of course, she wanted me to do the talking, but that's Naomi. For her it was just cheap entertainment. Em thought we should leave well enough alone. She said the whole thing made her want to vomit and if I didn't watch out I was going straight to jail. For once Em and Naomi were in agreement.

Naomi threatened to turn me in if I didn't fill out another change of address card to send the mail back immediately. She watched me do it, sitting at my dining room table bitching and drinking without coasters since Em was out. Our glasses left dark rings on the light wood. Em had stripped and refinished the table for me and was very particular about it even after giving it away. She suspected that every time she went out more rings appeared on its face. She was, of course, right, as I could never find the coasters and Naomi wouldn't use them anyway. Naomi said it was up to me whether or not to tell Bev about Kelsey's affair.

That had been two months ago and I was still procrastinating. Fortunately Bev was beating me to the punch by sitting in the Penguin telling me she knew about the affair.

I asked Bev again how she knew and almost choked on my beer when she said she'd been reading Kelsey's mail.

"Kelsey doesn't know I know about her affair." Bev sipped her wine. The wine must have been as bad as I expected because she made a face and pushed the glass away.

She took a breath. "She gets her mail in her own box for the upstairs apartment, but I have the key. She was working late and I thought it would be nice to have it waiting up there since I was sleeping in her apartment that night," Bev explained. "Sometimes she's tired and we sleep apart."

Bev had found the card with the rest of the mail. I remembered the handwriting style and didn't have to ask how she knew to open it.

"Do you need a place to stay for a while?" I asked and was guilty that I felt relief when she told me she could manage. Three women in a two-bedroom condo with one bathroom is a trial no matter how close you are.

"Thanks for listening," she said. She really looked like she meant it. "I haven't decided what I'm going to do. I might need to call you."

"Anytime," I said. As rotten as it sounds, I was glad to have my best friend back even under the circumstances. I wasn't glad to have been right about Kelsey but I figured Bev would get over her in the long run. She'd recovered from all the other romantic bruises in her life and, like they say, in the long run we're all dead. What worried me was getting her through the short-term pain which, I thought, might be pretty bad when the shock wore off.

Bev bent her head to kiss me on the cheek. I thought she was going to say something else but instead she just walked out of the bar. My watch said it was 12:35 am and I felt too tired to sleep so I had another beer before I headed home.

IV

My alarm went off at five-thirty the next morning. Em has it set so she can get up and run her five miles before breakfast. I hit the snooze button and was late for work again. Em never let me oversleep like that. She set multiple alarms for me when she was home. I thanked God that she was due back on Friday from her seminar and that when I rolled into the office at 11:30 my boss, the Irishman, had called in sick. I thanked God again that Starr had covered for me, and made a mental note to buy her some flowers. I also promised myself to stop drinking for real this time.

I took the stack of phone messages, dropped them in the trash, and headed for my office. I would tell whoever called back that I never got the message. For lunch I had Diet Coke and M&M candy in my office with my door closed and my phone on Do Not Disturb. By two o'clock I'd gotten through my backlog of reports and sent it all to typing. I was safe for another week so I thought I'd kick back for a while. Starr knocked on my door and opened it before I could answer.

"You working?" she said. "I thought you were just hung over."

I laughed.

People were always sleeping one off in their offices at Whytebread. You could close your door and take a little nap if the world was spinning a little too feverishly. For some of my colleagues this happened frequently, but it hadn't seemed to hurt their careers, while mine was going nowhere fast. Whytebread and Greese was a sleepy little investment firm. Far from the hustle and bustle of Wall Street was how we liked to characterize it. Outsiders might, however, describe it as second tier if they were being kind — third tier if they embraced brutal honesty. Small potatoes.

Whytebread had been, until the mid-80s stock market boom, a welfare institution for old white men from the North Shore. A guy could make a nice living for his family here, keep a flask in his bottom drawer for entertainment and die peacefully behind his desk from sclerosis of the liver after a big lunch at the Chicago Club. Suddenly the markets boomed like a high tide raising all the ships and we were in the game. That startled the old men who ran the firm. Then, as if Adam Smith's own invisible hand had shaken them awake, they figured out how much money they could be making. They hired all the MBA's they could find from fancy schools, my own included, to make the money for them since they had no idea how to do it themselves. In the same way that people welcome migrant workers into town at harvest time, they needed so many minds to tap the market that for a while nobody cared if you weren't white. So, Whytebread hired me with my expensive education and my accentless speech along with the usual white boys. And my cohorts and I pretended that we really knew how to make them rich.

"I took some aspirin," I admitted to Starr.

"Well, your friend Naomi called ten times," said Starr. "So maybe you should call her." She closed the door hard.

Starr wasn't really nasty, just efficient and unsentimental. Inside she was a sweet girl with a wall of lipstick and bleached-out hair built around her vulnerability. She kept a picture of her baby brother in a frame on her desk next to a stuffed teddy bear.

I got Naomi on the speaker phone after one ring.

"Where have you been?" Naomi said. "I've been calling you all day. Have you read the papers?"

The *Trib* and the *Journal* were still in my briefcase. "No. I got in late. Was I supposed to?" I was worried that the market had tanked again. I couldn't afford to be out of a job anytime soon.

Naomi blew out her breath in exasperation. "Well for Godsakes look at them, Ginny."

I pulled my case off the chair beside my desk. It was a stretch without getting up. I get tired of Naomi's flair for the dramatic and wanted her to just tell me in simple English what was going on. "Everything is a fire drill with you," I said.

"Just read the fucking paper, all right?" said Naomi. "The city section on the second page."

The headline read: Executive Killed in Possible Gaybashing near Lesbian Bar. The story featured an inset picture of Kelsey looking like the future of American Business in a dark suit and pearls, along with a shot of a space in the alley behind Gloria's Place where a body had presumably been. She had been shot repeatedly according to the article. The police hypothesized gaybashing from the viciousness of the attack and the proximity to Gloria's, or robbery, or both. The neighborhood around Gloria's wasn't exactly the kind of place where people sign up for the Neighborhood Watch. People got beat up all the time, sometimes gay people, sometimes not. The police had no suspects.

"Jesus." I felt like someone had punched me in the stomach. I had never known anyone who had died violently — no one young. I asked Naomi where Bev was.

Her voice sounded like it was coming from inside a tin can. She blew her smoke out into the phone. "I don't know, Virginia, but we could have a real problem here."

Naomi knew a U.S. attorney who said that the

Feds had been investigating Kelsey and some work crony of hers, Jim Nealy, for embezzlement. They weren't so sure Kelsey's death was robbery.

Naomi groaned. "Do you know what I can look forward to if it comes out that I knew this woman socially? They'll send me back to felony review." Naomi hated felony review — where our judicial system decides at all hours of the night whether there is enough evidence to charge violent criminals. Years ago Naomi worked the 11:00 pm to 7:00 am graveyard shift until her father made a phone call. "I can count the number of gay judges with no fingers and no toes," she whined.

I still didn't understand. If Kelsey had embezzled enough money to interest the U.S. attorney, where was it? I was intimate with Kelsey's bank accounts. They had looked pretty distressed to me and if she wasn't strapped for cash, why did she need Bev? Naomi didn't have those answers so her superior attitude was really starting to frost me.

"Look," I said, "why do we have a problem? We didn't kill her. At least I didn't kill her." It was a joke, but Naomi didn't laugh.

"When regular people get killed, the spouse or the lover did it," Naomi said authoritatively. "If the Feds have been watching Kelsey, they know she and Bev are lovers. They'll know Kelsey was cheating. Maybe they'll think they were partners in the embezzlement scheme. Maybe they *were* partners in the embezzlement scheme. I don't know, but it's bad for us. That's for sure."

What Naomi had said struck me as pretty uncharitable and I got annoyed.

"Maybe Kelsey deserved it," she said, trying to

smooth my feelings. "I really don't know. I never liked Kelsey anyway. Don't take it personally, all right?"

"How am I supposed to take it?" Naomi had no tact, just savvy. I was getting more annoyed by the minute and I wasn't understanding Naomi at all.

She laughed like breaking glass. "It's going to be a sad day for us mainstream middle-class lesbians if this sucker goes to trial."

Naomi was hysterically worried that either of us, but mostly she, could be called as a witness if Bev was prosecuted for Kelsey's murder. I thought Naomi was getting way ahead of herself.

"If Bev is prosecuted for Kelsey's murder, we'll do everything we can to get her off, right?" I said. "That's all, we'll get her off."

"How is it going to play at Whytebread and Greese?" Naomi demanded. "Do you think you're ever going to make partner after the *Times* writes the screaming headline: Black Investment Banker Testifies in Lesbian Love Triangle Homicide? If Bev calls me to get her out of jail I might as well just resign. And I don't even want to think about the mail tampering. I should have turned you in, it'd be one less thing to worry about."

"Thanks a lot." I made a note not to call Naomi if I were ever in trouble with the law.

"You know what I mean." I could hear Naomi smoking into the phone.

"Relax," I said. "Bev didn't kill Kelsey. How do you even know she will be charged? The police can't arrest people for no reason."

Naomi took a deep breath which I took to mean she was starting from the very beginning for my benefit and that it exasperated her. "The police need probable cause to arrest someone. All that is, is what a reasonable person would take as evidence to believe that someone could have committed a crime. That Kelsey and Bev were lovers contributes enough to probable cause that the cops would certainly look into Bev's motives. Jealousy is one of the best motives I know — that and money. Could Bev get any money out of this?" she asked.

"For Godsakes, Naomi," I said.

"Well, it was just a thought." Naomi sighed. "Once you're arrested all your constitutional rights kick in. There has to be a hearing and then a trial. Are you with me?" she asked.

I made noises like I was hanging on her every word, but it seemed to me that if Bev got charged with murder there were more things to worry about than my prospects for partner. The main thing was to get her off. You can't let a friend go to jail to keep your name out of the papers — well, I couldn't, anyway.

"If the prosecutor wants to prove that Bev killed Kelsey," Naomi continued.

"Of course, she didn't kill Kelsey," I said irritably. "She was with me last night."

"That may be so." Naomi paused and started again more loudly to demonstrate that she was in the right. "But if the prosecutor wants to prove that Bev killed Kelsey, he has to have some kind of motive. All the cops have to do is get a search warrant for Kelsey's apartment and find more of those lovely epistles from that girlie, Mary, in Boston. The prosecutor doesn't have to be a rocket scientist to dig us up and force us to testify to Bev's lesbianism and by implication probably our own."

"I think you're getting a little ahead of yourself, Naomi," I said reasonably. "Has Bev even been charged? How is he going to find you anyway if you don't come forward?"

"Lots of ways, address books, neighbors. You used to hang out at Bev's all the time. The more sensational a crime," Naomi asserted, "the more the newspapers want to investigate all of its nooks and crannies. I think a bunch of upscale lesbians and their friends involved in a love triangle might sell some copy don't you?" Naomi made her brittle laugh.

"You have to do what you have to do, Naomi," I said. "But if it came to all that, maybe it would help Bev if we testified." I asked if Naomi thought Bev needed a lawyer right now.

"Of course," Naomi said, "that's what I've been saying, if you want to help Bev, keep her out of jail and help us all, okay?"

Sometimes I don't like Naomi, but if things were as bad as she thought they were, a lawyer made sense to nip the whole thing in the bud. It was for sure that Bev hadn't killed Kelsey as far as I was concerned and there was no sense in her getting harassed over it. I had an idea of how the cops might treat the remaining half of a lesbian couple. Besides, I didn't even want to think about being front page news.

There was a human rights ordinance in the city to keep you from getting fired for being gay or lesbian, but it couldn't get you promoted and it didn't pay your bonus at the end of the year. And there are ways to make you quit without firing you and without breaking the law. I would rather not have it come to that; I'd worked too hard. Not just for myself. My family had educated me for a reason. My view of the lake meant something to my father, a man whose people came north in the steel migration of the 1940s, and to my mother whose parents believed in the 1960s that she had married a man too dark to provide for her and their progeny.

Naomi gave me the number of a trial lawyer she knew from school. I wrote the name, Susan Coogan, down carefully on a Post-it and stuck it to the inside flap of my briefcase. Naomi sounded happy that I was finally being what she considered reasonable.

"You see that this has got to be contained for everybody's sake," she said. "You should probably call Bev today. Tell her I'm sorry. If they pick her up, Susan will bail her out. But I can't afford to get any calls from a lockup. Working for the State, I couldn't help her out anyway."

I still had a terrific headache. Bev's office told me she was at home. The phone rang a long time before she answered which didn't help my head any. I told her I had read about Kelsey and I was sorry. I asked how she was, but she didn't sound good.

"The police were here this morning," she said, "and I was sleeping when you called."

Bev had tried to go into work but couldn't get it together. She had decided last night to leave Kelsey but Kelsey wasn't home when she'd gotten in so she couldn't tell her. Bev had gone on to bed in her downstairs apartment. Then the police were knocking on the door at five o'clock in the morning with a search warrant for Kelsey's apartment. They unceremoniously informed Bev that her landlady was dead, and asked if she had another key to upstairs. Kelsey's wallet had been fished out of a dumpster behind a Gloria's: no cash, no keys, but there was ID and they wanted to search Kelsey's apartment so could she let them in.

I told her again how sorry I was and asked if there was anything I could do.

Bev caught her breath to keep from crying. "This has been so awful," she said. "I can barely think of anything past this minute." Her voice was hoarse and cracked and I listened while she cried into the phone. But after a while she seemed to get herself together. She asked me to excuse her. Then she said there was something I could do, if I didn't mind, but she'd tell me when I got there.

I promised to stop by that afternoon. It didn't seem like the right time to mention the lawyer, so I didn't.

The clock in my office said 3:30 pm. I put the newspapers in my bag and told Starr I was leaving for the day. She was putting florescent pink polish on her nails. She smiled knowingly when I said I had a stomach flu, which was close to the truth since my hangover was debilitating. Still, I was beginning to think that Starr listened to my phone conversations on the conference line.

I had taken the car to work that day since I was so late. I drove home up Lakeshore Drive with the top down, grateful to see the sun. It had been the wettest August I could remember, but today was clear. The lake was very smooth and blue.

I thought of a piece of trivia I had read somewhere about the filming of *The Graduate*. It took my mind off Kelsey. Mike Nichols, when he filmed *The Graduate,* stopped traffic on the Bay Bridge so that Dustin Hoffman could drive backwards on the open-topped part from San Francisco to Oakland in order to begin the film with that long blue aerial shot of a young Dustin Hoffman in his imported car and miles of open road going from one part of his life to another. Real people driving from San Francisco to Oakland drive on the lower Bay Bridge which is covered, grey and industrial with not much view. Maybe it was designed that way to prepare you for Oakland.

That day, Lakeshore Drive was wide open, four lanes across one way, and I could not feel nearly as sad as I should have. The lakefront is like that. When there are sailboats in the water and the sun is out, it's hard to believe that anything could be wrong. That's why people live in Chicago; on a summer day, you forget that winter will ever come. That afternoon, I felt as good as Dustin Hoffman in that movie, with the sun on my head, the wind roaring around my ears and at least fifty safe, happy middle-class years ahead of me. Melissa Etheridge was cranked up loud on my tape deck, singing about "Similar Features" or it seemed to me some other heartbreak. The bass shook the car, but in the wind I could barely hear it.

Bev's house was on the way home if I took the North Avenue exit. She hugged me as I came in.

"Just tell me what I can do to help," I said.

"I'm just so afraid," Bev said and I asked her why. She still looked pretty broken up and I wondered if something else had happened, but she told me no.

"There's a gun here that was Kelsey's," Bev said. "She gave it to me to keep down here in this apartment for safety when I sleep alone. I'd like it if you'd just keep it for a while until they find whoever did this."

"Why not get rid of it?" I suggested.

But Bev insisted she was sentimental about the thing since Kelsey had given it to her. She opened the bottom drawer of her kitchen cabinets and pulled it out from under some dish towels.

Bev put the gun out on the kitchen counter. There are gun people and non-gun people. I like to think of myself as the latter. I don't like guns. Gun people, suffice it to say, gun people will shoot you. All I know about guns I learned from a cop I used to date. This one was a small automatic, silver and squared-off. It was a wimpy gun as guns go. I didn't know much about guns, but I looked at the butt to see if it was loaded like my cop ex-girlfriend showed me. She was a gun person. She used to leave her gun on my dining room table when she stopped by for sex which was the primary focus of our relationship. That was before Emily. The arrangement had had an attractive simplicity that I was starting to miss.

"It's an unloaded gun," I said. "Just put it back in the drawer."

"Then you won't take it?" Bev asked me.

I handed it back to her. "I'd rather not. I don't like guns."

She put it back in the drawer under the towels. "If it can't be fired, I won't worry."

I assured her that unloaded guns did not go off and she seemed satisfied, though I wondered out loud why Kelsey would give her an unloaded gun for safety.

"Don't you have any bullets for this gun?" I asked.

Bev got them from the top shelf of the linen closet and brought them to me. She suggested: "Maybe you could just take these, then."

I didn't want the ammunition either. "If you just keep the gun and ammunition apart, I think you'll be pretty safe," I said.

That seemed to suit her. Bev actually looked better than she had the night before. She had been crying but the dark circles were gone. I sat down on a stool at the breakfast bar in her kitchen and said again how sorry I was. I felt so sad that I started to cry.

It is surprising that you can cry over the death of someone you didn't care for, but then I cried every night watching the evening news. For those godless ones of us who have left our faith behind in our childhoods, there is no afterlife to give us peace; and in death, it seems that all the attributes of individuality — humor, anger, hope — are dropped down a deep black hole with the bodies, scattered with the ashes on the ground. Those of us born to a generation that has seen too many miracles of science cannot imagine what has not been seen or reported on electronically, and are left without the comfort of heaven. I cried for myself, wiping my nose with the back of my hand, drinking in gulps the herbal tea that Bev had made for me, feeling strangely embarrassed at my sadness.

Her apartment was dark and sad, large and claustrophobic at the same time because so little light came in from outside. The windows were small and only along one wall. The developer had spent his money on things like skylights for the upstairs place. Bev's apartment was rental property, an afterthought to the owner's unit, but she had fixed it up really nice. It was homey with stuff from her old place when she lived alone, and I had liked it there.

"I'm sorry, Bev," I said, and tried unsuccessfully to laugh. "I should be comforting you, not the other way around."

She shook her head. "Oh, honey, I'm all cried out. That's all," she said. "After Kelsey told me about that woman, things don't seem real anymore."

I blew my nose and nodded. She was right. Things didn't seem real at all. My life was starting to feel like a movie with me standing outside watching, and not a good movie either, not one with a happy ending. Just like in the movies, I couldn't help asking Bev what exactly had happened with her and Kelsey. The subject had all the fascination of a traffic fatality on the freeway when you know not to look but at the last minute cannot help yourself.

Bev looked as if I'd balled up my fist and hit her in the face. "Are you saying you think I killed Kelsey?" She poured the leftover water from the tea down the sink and let the kettle smack on the counter when she put it down.

I wasn't saying that at all. "No. I was just wondering what happened, that's all."

"A friend wouldn't need to ask me that," said Bev, and I didn't like the implication. But she told me that she and Kelsey had had a fight before she called me for a drink. She swore the fight hadn't been at Gloria's, though. They had fought over the card in Kelsey's apartment after dinner. Kelsey had left to go she didn't know where and Bev had sat downstairs by herself in the dark until she called me to meet her. The police had taken a statement, but they hadn't asked if she and Kelsey were lovers and Bev hadn't volunteered it. She was angry and hurt and I couldn't blame her.

But I said: "Why didn't you tell me you'd had a fight when we talked at the Penguin last night?"

Bev looked me square in the face. "Last night you were drunk," she said. "How much good would your advice have been?"

I didn't remember being drunk, but if she meant that it was a good thing I'd walked home, I supposed she was right. I felt pretty small when I thought I might not have been capable of giving her my whole attention and that I'd put my foot in it again. "Look," I said, "I'm not trying to interrogate you. You don't have to tell me this if you don't want."

Bev set her hands on her hips and squared her shoulders. On her, the tough guy stance was nearly laughable, but she got it across that she wasn't kidding. "I'll tell you what I told the police," she said. "The last time I saw Kelsey was when she left here at nine last night." Then she began to cry again, and her mascara ran. She looked badly painted.

I told her I wasn't saying she had killed Kelsey, but that Naomi was afraid the police would think so. I tried to explain how bad that would be if she got arrested, but it sounded mostly like I was worried about myself even to me. The more I talked the worse it sounded. When I offered her the defense lawyer's number, she handed the paper right back to me without looking at it.

"I think you'd better leave now, Ginny," she said, and it seemed to me there was no use fighting.

I picked up my briefcase and walked out. Bev closed the door as soon as I was over the threshold. I heard the deadbolt turn behind me and I felt like shit.

VI

There was a message from Naomi on my machine. It was short and stressed, promising to pick me up for dinner and demanding that I be waiting for her in front of my apartment.

We drove down side streets for a half an hour until Naomi finally gave up and put her car by a hydrant near Addison. By the time we took a walk down the gay strip of Broadway and two blocks over to the Halsted Diner, we might as well have walked from my place. But Naomi likes to drive and she used the walk to fill me in.

She had made the rounds all afternoon panning for nuggets of information. I was afraid to guess how many favors she had called in, but she was chain-smoking her Marlboros down to the filters.

We got a booth and the waitress came over right away. I like the waitresses at the Halsted Diner. They're career waitresses as opposed to part-time actresses with the dyed black hair and the black clothes who are biding time before they move to New York and pick up their Tony awards. You can count on a career waitress to get the order right and just bring your food without any attitude. Our waitress was real Diner with a chest that spilled over her stomach and a white cotton uniform stretched tight across her butt. In her face, she looked about seventy-five years old, but her eyes sized us up for the tip and she wrote our orders down with a minimum of chat. I had the hamburger plate with the thick-cut fries and a beer. My relatives have all died of strokes and hypertension and I don't imagine there is anything I can do to thwart my genetics. Naomi had some black coffee and picked at the bread in a basket on the table.

"Things aren't looking good, Gin." She rubbed her forehead and sighed. "This seems to have become a case people want to solve — not just the Feds, either."

Naomi lit a cigarette and set the pack on the table beside her. She told me how the District Attorney, Halligan, had had a public shouting match with Jose Alvarez from the Gay and Lesbian Task Force not too long ago. But that was old news and even I had heard it. All the gay papers had reported it front page. Halligan had come all the way up to

59

the Northside to court the upscale gay and lesbian vote over drinks and nouvelle catering. Of course, the boys loved it. Halligan needed to be courting the gay and lesbian community. A lot of us weren't so sure he was doing his job where we were concerned. I, for one, was ready to express my displeasure in the voting booth. Lately, two guys had been beaten up on the way home from a bar in my neighborhood and that was just lately. Gaybashing was on the rise. We civilian queers weren't feeling so safe in our old hangouts and the Task Force wanted the DA to do something about it. Jose called him out at the meeting for being soft on hate crimes. It made the straight local news too, which is something in a town where the newspapers won't cover the Gay Pride Parade, and Halligan was embarrassed. According to Naomi, he was coming down hard on this because of elections in November, but would love to be able to write the whole thing off as some gay-on-gay crime of passion if he could. He'd said as much to his assistant DAs.

Then there was the matter of the Feds. Naomi's friend in the U.S. Attorney's office said their eyebrows were raised all the way up to their hairlines because Kelsey had happened to get murdered before they could indict her. The U.S. Attorney's Office was counting on Kelsey to roll over on her partners and their theory was that Kelsey's partners, whoever they were, had killed her to keep her quiet. Kelsey had been killed with a small caliber bullet like a .22. Professionals use a .22 because the smaller caliber bullet drives splinters of bone into the brain for a surely fatal head shot. But whoever killed Kelsey was angry and had emptied the gun into her pretty randomly. She was shot in the head and face as well as the body at close range, maybe four feet, as if someone had taken shots blindfolded, and some of the wounds looked like they'd been made after she was already down. So, the cops hadn't ruled out a robbery gone sour or gaybashing since it was right near a lesbian bar in a pretty marginal neighborhood, which was sending Halligan through the ceiling.

"This is the thing," said Naomi. "The police think Nealy might have done it. They're thinking maybe he and Kelsey had a falling out over money, something, but Nealy's in Boston and Kelsey was killed sometime between nine that night and two in the morning. So, Nealy's got to fly here from Boston and fly back in time for work. The earliest flight gets into Logan at nine-ten am and he was late to work today, but it would still be pretty tight." Naomi exhaled smoke through her nose. "The other thing is that the girl from Boston Kelsey was cheating with, Mary Tally, is a clerk in that same office. She works for Nealy."

That was interesting. "Yeah?" I said.

Naomi raised her eyebrows. "She was late this morning too."

"How late?"

Naomi grinned. "Late enough."

"What about Bev?" I asked.

"I haven't heard anything, but they've got to know about her and Kelsey. If the police know about Mary Tally, then they have a motive and you and me have still got trouble."

"Fine," I said. "Tell me something good."

Naomi smiled for the first time all night. "The good news in this is nobody has said a thing about Kelsey's mail being diverted. I don't think they were watching her mail, just her bank accounts."

"Thank God," I said. "Because we've got other problems with Bev." I ran my fingers through the front of my hair like a pick. "Bev won't take Susan Coogan's number. She tossed me out of her apartment for trying to give it to her."

"What?" That didn't make Naomi any happier.

I shrugged. "I don't know what we're going to do about it."

Naomi sat with her head in her hands while I filled her in on what Bev had said about the night Kelsey died.

"Great, Ginny. Who the fuck is she going to call when they arrest her?"

"I don't know. Maybe they won't." I was cutting my hamburger in two for easier handling and it was taking most of my attention. I covered it and my fries with ketchup. The other thing I like about the Halsted Diner is the ketchup always looks pretty new. I don't know how they manage that. The news about the mail-tampering had taken a load off my mind and I was hungry. I eyed the desserts in the case by the door and decided on the German chocolate cake.

Naomi groaned. "How can you eat? Of course they're going to arrest her and it will be worse since she lied in her statement."

"She didn't lie. They just didn't ask her if she and Kelsey were lovers. Maybe they won't find out," I offered. "Maybe they think Kelsey's partner, that

Nealy guy, killed her or maybe she just got mugged. If everyone killed women who cheated on them, there would be a lot of dead bodies. Even the cops must realize that. Relax," I said.

"I can't relax." Naomi dug another Marlboro out of the pack and stuck it in her mouth. "Look at me. I'm too stressed. This is my career, you know. I haven't got a whole hell of a lot else in my life." She had a point. Naomi lived to work.

"You know, Naomi," I said, "you smoke too much and I don't think the coffee helps."

She ignored me. "Look," she said, "it can't hurt to call Susan, Ginny. If Bev won't call a lawyer why don't you be a friend and call one for her. I'd do it, really, but I can't risk getting that involved."

Naomi was begging. I liked that.

"All right." It seemed inconceivable that I could piss Bev off much more than I had already and maybe she was going to need to talk to someone. I looked at it as covering my bets.

"Besides, you'll like Susan." Naomi took a sip of her coffee. "I guarantee it."

I liked Naomi much better when she was happy.

VII

Susan Coogan's office was only a block from my own which cinched it. I met her there after work on Friday. It was 6:30 pm but she was still working. Papers were spread all over her desk. She didn't look up when the secretary showed me in and closed the door.

"Have a seat. I'll be with you in a second," she said.

I sat in the chair across from her desk and watched her read. She wet her finger every time she turned a page. The waiting was a game to let me know she was a busy woman and I was lucky she'd made time for a nobody like me. The chair where I sat was pure old men's club, leather with buttons all over it. It let me know her time billed at big bucks to afford the upholstery.

A lot of professional offices make you feel like you've been caught in a time warp. Law offices are usually the worst. Everything is designed to look old and staid, if possible antique, optimally English. This works well for gray-haired relations of the founding partners, but women outside of the Junior League and minorities of any gender tend to look a little put-on against the backdrop of dark wood and Currier and Ives. Sometimes radical associates will try to assert their individuality — a Cubs cap on the bookcase, a bulletin board filled with feminist cartoons, a framed award for outstanding service from the Urban League, small signs of protest against the homogeneity of the large corporate firm. In my own office at Whytebread I had hung a small signed print by a local black artist, a lithograph of a black girl in a white dress and a field of flowers. It had been received with polite silence which I chose to take as consent.

Susan Coogan had surrendered to the blue blood ambiance of her white shoe law firm. All she needed for that office to belong to some geriatric founder was a brass reading lamp and some woodsy print of guys shooting at ducks. She had substituted a kind of quasi-impressionist thing on the wall of her office, a signed print with a low number. The print was big, replete with pastels and tiny brush strokes, and yet still really stuffy. I was sure she had picked the print carefully, viewing it as a strategic nod to femininity, but just a nod.

"Interesting reading?" I asked.

She showed me straight white teeth and told me, "Very."

I admit that I liked Susan with her plain, tanned face and bowl-cut blonde hair, clearly a color that was not her own. The details of Susan's features, the set of her eyes and the size of her nose didn't quite fit; seeing one, you would not presume the other. But the overall effect was not unpleasant. Susan had the sex-appeal of homely women who know that at the bottom line, in the dark, their looks don't matter. There was a general invitation in her smile.

Today she wore an expensive suit that said, in bold type and large font, CAREER DYKE. The styling was borrowed from Barbara Stanwyck when she played that lesbian madam in *Walk on the Wild Side* and I imagined Susan sat open-legged behind her desk. Apparently no one had told her that dresses were making a comeback in the courts and boardrooms of America. But somehow I didn't peg Susan Coogan as a slave to fashion.

"I'm sorry." She gave me another broad view of her large, perfect teeth. "I had to finish that or risk losing my train of thought. What can I do for you?" she said, moving her papers to clear a place on her desk. She folded her hands in a listening stance. She was a professional listener.

I told her my name again and that I was a friend of Naomi's. Susan smiled broadly. She figured I was a dyke; all the women Naomi knew were dykes.

66

"Naomi mentioned you as someone I should look up if I ever needed a lawyer," I said.

"And do you need a lawyer?" She took two metal balls from a case on her desk and rolled them in the palm of one hand like Captain Queeg who I remembered from sophomore English class.

"No," I said, "but a friend of mine does. I think the police are going to arrest her for murder."

"Why do you think that?" Her expression was practiced and faintly amused. She had these discussions all the time and for the most part they bored her. In this one, she saw the potential for a little entertainment.

I shrugged and repeated my story of the housewarming and the mail and the trip to Bev's. I omitted the facts that Bev had thrown me out of her apartment and that I didn't know if she'd accept any help from me at all, let alone let me pick a lawyer to defend her. That complicated the story. I had decided suddenly that I cared what this woman thought of me and I wanted her to see my good side. Susan worked the balls contemplatively in her hand and they made a faint ringing sound as they rubbed together. When I had finished, the ringing was the only sound in the office.

"You tell me," I said. "Does my friend need a lawyer?"

Susan put her toys back in their case and folded her hands over her desk. She had a French manicure. "That depends," she said evenly. "But why don't you let me buy you dinner and we'll talk about how much this is going to cost."

We ate at an Italian place in River North. Before dinner, she walked me around through the artsy district under the El tracks west of LaSalle, chatting me up about what painters and galleries she thought were good. She took me to a place that handled Native American artists where she kissed the proprietor and recited credits. Susan was on mailing lists; she went to openings; it was her hobby to be smart and know who'd painted what. Em would not let me buy art with my savings. In her practical immigrant way, she said real estate was a better investment.

The restaurant was a huge warehouse with open tables and an accordion player who did requests. The fare was kind of nouvelle, but the entrees had familiar pronunciations and the prices were affordable. I had the seafood linguine and a beer the waiter claimed was from Italy. Susan never got around to discussing her fee schedule. She talked, instead, relentlessly about herself and her failed relationships. There were many and she started the evening on the topic of her first. Most recently, her lover had walked out after two years.

"I cried a lot when Tina left," Susan said. "Now I work all the time to take my mind off it."

"That sounds terrible," I said in polite commiseration.

"It is." She laughed to show me that she didn't need my sympathy and then proceeded to go fishing for it. "I haven't gotten out in weeks."

Susan lamented her life as an associate. For the first year, all she did was photocopy documents from seven am until one in the morning. She was still working the same kind of hours but at least she was doing trial work. She closed her eyes as though she lived to go to trial. "At first Tina always waited up for me," she said. "But after a while, she was usually gone when I got home. I guess that should have been a tip-off." She stirred cream and sugar into her coffee absently.

"I'm sorry," I said, though she seemed to have gotten over it.

The accordion player broke into a corny old song near our table and I was charmed when Susan knew all of the words. She had a nice alto voice and the man clapped for her when she was done. Some of the other tables clapped too.

"Are you crazy?" I asked.

"Yes," she admitted. "It's why Tina left." Then she laughed.

I laughed too and thought she was witty. Her quirky looks were growing on me.

"You must know you have beautiful eyes," Susan said. It was an old line she must have used a lot. Her voice was romantic and tired at the same time, as if she were anxious to get to the good parts of a book she liked and had read before. It was time to mention that I lived with Em.

"Thank you," I said instead. "That's a very nice thing to say."

"My pleasure," said Susan. "Really."

After a while, she called for the check and seemed pleased that I didn't fight with her over it. But if the truth be told, it wasn't in my week's allowance. Susan promised that if the police arrested Bev which she doubted, since they hadn't even questioned her, she would be Bev's counsel if that was what Bev wanted. Susan didn't ask for any money. She explained that Bev had to hire her. That was all she would promise without talking to Bev.

We made an unrelated date for lunch the following week.

Susan drove me to my building. We shook hands goodbye in her car where she tried to hold both my gaze and my hand for longer than if she was just being chummy. Before I could get out of the car, she pulled me back over to her seat and kissed me. It was wet, but nice. She was embarrassed, then, and she looked away while I opened the door to go. I took my time walking through the courtyard to my steps and when I turned Susan was still double-parked, blocking traffic, waiting to see that I got into the foyer okay.

Em was reading with her feet up, history. She never read fiction; she craved facts.

Em worried that she lacked exposure, having grown up in a neighborhood on the Northwest Side that none of her relatives had ever left, and she took evening classes at a local college in anything that struck her fancy, sometimes science, sometimes history. I liked to take her to couples parties where they played those games of trivia because she always won.

Her legs were crossed at the ankles over her crew socks. Em wore running shoes constantly, even around the apartment. The soles left marks on the coffee table. I never wear shoes at all if I can help it. There is already enough structure in my life.

The room was dark except for the reading light on the end table by the couch and the blinds were up so that I could see into my neighbors' apartments. No one was home.

Em didn't bother to look up from her book.

"Where have you been?" she asked me, more out of politeness than interest.

"I had dinner with Naomi." I can't tell you why I lied to her. Perhaps the charm of little secrets kept from your lover. It had been a long time since anyone besides Em had bought me dinner. "Naomi and I had dinner," I said again.

"Oh," Em said, "that's nice." Her eyes never left her text on the Spanish-American war. "The cat threw up again."

I stood behind her and kissed her neck, but she could not be distracted. "He has hair balls," I whispered. When Em said nothing, I added, "I'm going to bed," meaning it as an invitation. "Are you coming soon?"

Em grunted. "I have another chapter," she said finally.

I picked up Sweet Potato, my cat, who was wound around my legs, and kissed him in front of his ears where his hair was thinning. Sweet Potato always wanted my affection. He was all of the things I would have liked Em to be: his feet were warm in bed and he was always happy to see me.

I carried him limp and purring into the bedroom. Then I closed the door and called Naomi. I woke her up and she was annoyed.

"Do you know what time it is?" she demanded.

I didn't. I told her that Susan had promised to bail Bev out if she needed it. I skipped the part about the dinner date.

"Great," said Naomi. "That's one less headache." But she was beginning to think that the police might not arrest Bev after all. Murder had no statute of limitation but as near as she could tell from the DA grapevine, the police and the Feds thought there was only one girlfriend — the one in Boston, Mary Tally. Naomi reminded me that this Mary was an accounting clerk at Kelsey's company. She had stopped showing up for work after Kelsey was killed and nobody knew where she was. The Feds didn't know whether to look for another body or not.

They had been getting ready to indict the head accountant, Nealy, who they thought was Kelsey's partner, when he caught wind of it and hung himself in the men's room at work. His co-workers said he was an old-fashioned family man with problems — by way of an explanation for his stealing — big in the Knights of Columbus and he just couldn't take the strain.

Nealy had approved purchase orders for small amounts through the usual company channels. When the checks were cut, he'd white-out the original amounts and write in a bigger amount. Then he'd initial the change. Kelsey controlled audit and would cover his tracks. They'd embezzled nearly one hundred and fifty thousand dollars in the past nine months and had laundered it in a series of phony bank accounts, making deposits and withdrawals with an ATM card. The statements went to a post office box that was filled with unopened correspondence. It looked like nobody had ever been there to pick up the mail. The Feds were still watching the bank accounts, but the trail looked pretty cold. Mary Tally was their only living lead and she had vanished.

On that note Naomi advised me that she at least

had to work tomorrow, wished me a goodnight and hung up.

I sat up reading with Sweet Potato on my feet for a while. Em came to bed finally. She put herself in beside me without a word, curled up on her side, showing me her back.

"Are you sleepy?" I asked her.

Em turned over. She propped herself up on her elbow and smiled the way she used to smile when we were first together. "I'm very tired," she said. "Class ran late and I worked hard today."

Em kissed my neck and licked the inside of my ears by way of a compromise. I rubbed her back until she went to sleep, snoring happily. When I woke up the next morning my legs and arms were still curled up around her. I remember thinking what a nice way it was to wake up.

VIII

My boss, the Irishman, came back from lunch drunk. This was nothing unusual. He was a huge red-faced man with a crude sense of humor and a prickly skin of insecurity, middle-aged and taking stock of himself against his Wall Street peers, not measuring up. He was hard to like. But the Irishman's drunks always held suspense. He had two kinds. Sometimes he was jolly and sentimental, telling winding stories about his daughters and his sons and how he loved his third wife. Teary-eyed and hugging all of the associates, he would take me aside especially, saying how there were opportunities at Whytebread for someone like me as if I had grown up fatherless on public aid when instead I had come from the school that old John D. Rockefeller built for his own folks. And the Irishman would testify on his own rise from humble working-class beginnings into his great financial services horn of plenty. He had such blind belief in the American Dream, I almost liked him, then in his next breath he would disappoint me with a joke that ended in some ugly name.

His other kinds of drunks were epic and raging. In the way wild animals get into an interactive pattern, scratching at the ground or running in circles unable to stop themselves, the Irishman's brain would get stuck in a nasty drunken loop during which he poured obscenities out on his subordinates.

He extricated himself by passing out and waking up with no memory. You could never tell what kind of drunk it would be until you set him off. The good drunks came by default when he had gone home or fallen asleep in his office without incident.

The Irishman would drink alone but liked better to have company. He took all the associates out routinely, with an emotion that had disguised itself in his mind and in ours as generosity, sometimes to loud restaurant pubs, sometimes just to street festivals. He bought us all as much beer as we could drink on those afternoons and made us drink until the boys were so drunk they couldn't go back to the office. It was a test of manhood to keep up with him, an illustration of the superiority of men. The women were happily excused after the first few rounds, before the off-color jokes came out.

Working for the Irishman was accepting the ups and downs of his alcoholism as beyond your control, riding them to your own advantage, reading them the way that people say good sailors can read the sea. I had been successful more or less. I stayed out of his way unless there was a good reason for me to be in it. But the Irishman's tantrums were adding a dimension of stress to my life beyond what was usually requisite in my line of work. In the last year, I had started to sweat profusely at work no matter what the temperature. Nothing could stop it. As a result, my dry cleaning bills were ridiculous and my stomach was nearly always upset.

Today the Irishman was in a bad drunk. I locked myself away in my office and listened to him holler at Rupert, a white boy associate who was not fast enough to make his escape before the Irishman went into this afternoon's tirade. I had no sympathy for Rupert.

At the last Whytebread Christmas party, so drunk that he was barely able to form the words, Rupert had told me he would not be working at Whytebread if he didn't think he would be president one day. Rupert had been with Whytebread four years, one year longer than I had. There are some jobs I know I need not aspire to but I don't like it rubbed in my face. Later, Rupert had gotten drunker and swatted me on the ass, which the Irishman and the others thought was a hilarious and ingenious act. I ground the heel of my pump into the toe of Rupert's Florsheim loafer when no one was looking. I had decided then that we were enemies, though Rupert was too stupid to notice.

I tried to call Bev again. Her secretary took a message.

After the din in the halls wore down, I decided on a little walk to see what was up. The Irishman was sleeping, having worn himself out on Rupert, and Rupert was sitting in his office staring at his terminal. He called to me.

"Did you hear that just now?" he said. "That bastard called me stupid." He looked like he wanted to cry.

"I'm sorry, Rupert," I said and was surprised at myself. For a minute he was not my enemy. I stopped by the door of his office, I wanted him to see that I was bigger than he was. I wanted to see by way of curiosity what humiliation must feel like to someone who has not been socialized to expect it. His face was broken from the sting and the surprise, like a pie in the face from a scene in some old slapstick silent picture. I would have liked to explain that a pie in the face doesn't hurt any less when you see it coming. But it would have been a long conversation. I shook my head and kept walking.

"Can you believe that shanty son-of-a-bitch said that to me?" Rupert asked, still muttering behind me. "I'm going to remember this."

Ellen Borgia, a few offices down the hall from Rupert, was working — not very hard — when I knocked on her open door. A good thing about Ellen, her door was always open, she was always willing to shoot the breeze. The other good thing about Ellen, she never asked me who I was dating or proposed man-hunting trips after work like the other women did. She had the cynicism about men that comes from being over thirty-five, straight and unmarried. Ellen just said no to female bonding.

"Oh, good," she said, "I was looking for an excuse not to work."

"Then you're in luck." I sat down and crossed my legs, waiting for Ellen to entertain me with her views on the world.

She told me how much she liked the dress I was wearing and related a story of how an up-and-coming woman in our firm, who was not much to look at, had gotten drunk and made a pass at one of the other associates. He had rejected her and now she had a vendetta going against him.

Ellen yawned. "He should have just fucked her and then told everybody about it. She would have been a harmless joke. Now, look at the trouble she's causing him. Men are either stupid or gay." Ellen sighed and remarked that she hated gay men. Their sex disgusted her and she viewed their masculinity as a wasted resource. "If there were fewer gay men, getting married would be no problem."

Ellen was looking hard for a man. Everyday she felt older and less optimistic about her marriage prospects.

"I suppose it's even worse for you as a black woman, Virginia," Ellen said. The thought seemed to comfort her.

I nodded. I don't lie, but I don't tell the truth either. It's a reasonable compromise that doesn't keep me up nights.

"Would you ever marry a white man?" asked Ellen.

"No," I said.

She thought about that for a while. Then she said, "You could you know; you've got a lot going for you."

IX

Susan changed our second date from lunch to a late dinner the following Thursday. She wanted to pick me up at my apartment, but I told her I would meet her. So, she was standing out in front of Cornelias, a restaurant off Halsted, when I arrived. She was stocky like a fireplug with her wide-body shoulders propped up against the side of the building. She had the look of a junior prom date. Instead of a corsage, she gave me a hug and an earnest kiss on the cheek.

Susan had changed into jeans and a

trendy-looking blouse — presumably at her office, because she still had her briefcase hung over her shoulder. It was the first time I had seen her in civilian clothing and the flat shoes took a good three inches off her height. I hadn't realized how short she was. I won't say it was a disappointment, but I'll own it was a surprise.

Susan managed to get us seated in a dark corner, and devoted dinner to a discussion of her current court cases and past legal triumphs. All lawyers seem to keep egos to feed like hungry pets, but defense attorneys have the moral fervor of religious fundamentalists. Susan offered no surprises in this respect.

She let me know early in the evening that her firm did *pro bono* work for black people, who, she asserted, disenfranchised from and by the system, were offered few outlets besides gratuitous violence, and that she, herself, was willing to put her body on the line in the streets and the housing projects to see that poor criminals got the same legal advantages as rich ones. I wasn't so sure she was doing me any favors. But the subtext of this pronouncement was to alert me, lest I had doubts, that her politics were in the correct alignment to fuck me. She fairly frothed at the mouth with the strength of her liberal convictions, but intensity has its charms, and obsessiveness in a lover can be more than attractive.

Then, there was the promise of her name — Susan. Naomi had a theory about that name. Naomi has a theory about almost everything. If she doesn't, she'll make one up for the occasion. According to Naomi, Susans were a rollercoaster ride not to be missed. There is something in the naming of them that ensures thrills and unreliability. Think of the Susans you have known.

My sister was almost named Susan, but another girl baby born down the street a month before had been called Susan and my mother in her practicality didn't want there to be two on the same block. So my sister is named Adeline after our grandmother, a rock of good sense and old-fashioned dependability, and baby Susan down the street grew up wild and brimming with craziness.

Which would you rather have: craziness and passion, or order and peace? I had tired of peace, so after dinner I let Susan take me back to her apartment.

Susan lived in a downtown highrise near her office. Like her office, it was glass and steel. The view of the city from her bedroom windows was like coming in for a night landing at O'Hare Field in a glass elevator; and when she touched me, my stomach felt as if I'd dropped in freefall. I closed my eyes and Susan filled my mouth with her tongue. She rolled it over my own and ran the tip of it slowly along the backs of my teeth.

Susan laid her cheek on my stomach and licked my belly, priming me. She said, "I'll bet you taste like all the lovely things you've ever had to eat." She laughed. I couldn't tell if she was more delighted with me or with her little joke, but it didn't matter. Her laughter was soft and introverted, and her delight prefaced her expectations of what would come.

I was embarrassed and quiet. Talk makes me shy. Susan whispered into my hips. "I'll bet you're warm and sweet like hot chocolate with marshmallows melting on top of it," she said and laughed again.

I knotted my fingers in the brown roots of her hair. Her mouth was like cream and she kissed me wet and open with her tongue between my lips. My body closed around her fingers and I welcomed each of them with my sighs. Afterwards, she slept with her head between my breasts and her arms closed around my waist to prevent my escape.

A man I once knew from West Texas had an expression: Coyote ugly. There are single baggers where you'll put a paper bag over her head to take her out. There are double baggers where you'll put one bag over her head and another over your own in case hers comes off. There are triple baggers. They are the same as double baggers with a second safety bag over her head. The worst is Coyote ugly, where you will gnaw off your own arm to escape in the morning.

From the way Susan held me as she slept, I wondered if I hadn't better sneak out while I still could. But I have made a policy of ignoring my instincts. Besides, I couldn't move without waking her. In her grand passion she had managed to throw all the sheets off the bed and I was cold, but I had tired of order and the craziness wouldn't come until later. I did not think of Em until the next morning. By then it didn't matter.

The first time I made love I remember it was like swimming underwater. Time stood still. Since then, it has never been the same. There is no wonder in it anymore and the delight is short-lived. Now, there is a protocol and what will happen next is easy to anticipate. If I told you that Susan changed all that, I would be lying, but with her flattery she made me forget it for a while.

When my sister and I were ten and fourteen respectively, my mother started back to work. She had other things in her life then besides my father, me and Adeline. She did it for herself, to have her own money. We were proud of her. My father learned to cook, a limited menu. I wore my house key on a piece of thick yarn around my neck to school and my mother baked for us infrequently. When she did, it was an occasion of some note, a birthday, Thanksgiving.

In that same way, sex with Em is a sentimental treat. With Em, sex is the texture of warm bread, slow and thick with past emotion. With Susan, it was a snowball rolling downhill, always building and then after, deja vu on a street where I had never been before, walking easily towards someplace I knew well. I could tell it was someplace special, but I think you'd know better.

Susan was lying propped up on her elbows watching me when I woke up. She had been awake for a while. I didn't know she wore glasses. She smiled and kissed me. I didn't mind that she hadn't brushed her teeth.

"I'll call in sick today, if you will," she said.

I laughed. "What the hell," I said. "You only live once." I would have to leave work early to pick up Em at the airport anyway.

Susan offered me some coffee, but I could never stand the stuff. She went out to make it and then brought hers back to bed. She had an expensive bed. I hadn't noticed the size of it the night before. It was wooden, a modern style, low to the ground with drawers underneath and a headboard with shelves. Her room was clean, not just dust-free, but sterile. I would have wondered if she or anyone actually lived there, but she knew where everything was. I watched her sip her coffee without waiting until it was cool enough to drink. She grimaced, surprised that it was so hot and bitter. She watched me too over the top of her cup as if I were something new she'd bought for her apartment and she was trying to decide where I'd look best. After a while she put the cup on the floor and kissed me again, holding me down on the bed.

"Who does your cleaning?" I asked her seriously, wondering if I could convince Em we needed a cleaning lady. But Susan had other things on her mind and she told me so.

"Let's get up," I said. "Come on. Let's do something."

She put her hands between my legs, insisting. "This is exactly what I want to do today," she said. So we made love. I less enthusiastically than the night before. It bothered her, but not enough to stop.

"What's wrong?" she asked afterwards.

"Nothing," I said. "I'm just tired."

She kissed me on the forehead, then on the mouth, grinning widely, and lay back to take a nap while I read the paper.

We called in sick.

Later we walked along the beach at Belmont and sat down to rest on the rocks. It was mid-afternoon. The sun was hot on the back of my neck and I wished I had a hat. Susan wore some sweat pants cut off above the knee. They said University of

Oregon on the thigh. Her legs looked like they could hold up the world.

I said, "University of Oregon in Eugene? Is that where you went to school?" I had known someone else who went there, a woman I'd lost track of.

"I don't know if it's in Eugene. Somebody gave me these. I went to Northwestern," Susan told me.

I nodded. "What did you study there?"

"Government," she said.

It struck me as odd not to know that about her, until I remembered I didn't know anything else. Susan never asked me anything besides yes or no questions. She had found out what she needed to know.

There was no wind and the lake was still, like a sheet of bottle-green glass that you could walk across to Michigan.

"You know, I never thought I'd get over it when Tina left," Susan said. "You won't leave me will you, Gin?"

I thought she was getting ahead of herself. "Let's just agree this is nice for now," I said.

Her legs hung over the side of the rocks and her head was bent down watching the water.

"I think I see some fishes," she said after a while and pointed, but all I could see was the green water.

I have good eyes. When I was a kid I caught salamanders in a creek with water green all choked from algae on pasture land owned by families who'd been in town for a hundred years, marrying their neighbors until we were all cousins, the great grandchildren of slaves who'd come as servants and stayed as farmers. I wondered how Susan had gotten here.

I looked at my watch. "I have to go," I said. I gave her my card and on the back I wrote my home phone. "I'm easier to catch at the office. Why don't you just call me there."

I left to pick up Em at O'Hare. Susan hugged me goodbye. She didn't ask me where it was that I had to go.

I met her five or six times at her apartment after that. There were some lunches, some dinners, some weekends when Em was out of town and a couple of quickies in a leather chair pushed against her office door before Susan called me at home.

I had almost forgotten that she had the number and besides, I took for granted that Susan had guessed I was already involved. She had never been to my apartment and I always met her at the restaurants where we ate. I was also sure Em had guessed about the affair and accepted it as a trade-off for my good spirits. I was surprised on both counts, but what else is new.

It was 10:30 pm when Susan called. Em and I were in bed, not talking, not sleeping. It was too hot to sleep and we didn't talk much these days. The phone was an annoyance and it begged the issue of who would get up and turn up the fan in the window, but the machine was off. Em got the phone. If Em was surprised to hear Susan ask for me, she didn't let it show. She was controlled about that as with most things.

"It's for you," she said and handed me the phone. "I don't know who it is."

I got out of bed and took the call in the living room closing the door after myself, ostensibly so Em could sleep. Em watched me, sitting up in bed with her arms crossed over her chest. I held the phone by the cradle with my hand closed over the speaker so that Susan couldn't hear.

"It's the defense lawyer I got for Bev," I told Em through the crack in the door as I was leaving. "Remember, I told you?" But I had never told her. We both knew it.

I settled myself on the couch in the living room and took my hand off the speaker.

"Who was that?" Susan asked, meaning Em. "It's late." Meaning she didn't care who it was; when it was late I should be with her.

"That was my lover, Em."

I'm not proud of it, but I was tired and I didn't even do her the courtesy of lying. I knew all her bedroom tricks. Even kink gets old. Surprise and delight were no longer part of her repertoire and I was ready for her to become a secret smile to stretch across my face in my old age, but she could not believe it.

There was a long silence on the other end of the phone. Then Susan laughed. But she was not amused. "I don't believe this," she said, meaning why don't you keep lying to me.

"Believe what?" I watched my cat, Sweet Potato, sitting on the radiator cover. He was beating his tail up and down like a metronome, happy to have my company. I thought it was nice that someone was happy.

She laughed again. "I don't believe you're even asking me that."

Sweet Potato came to sit in my lap, stretching and yawning as he crossed the room. I scratched his head between his ears which is the place he likes best.

"She's black, isn't she?" Susan asked, meaning, "What does she have that I don't?"

"No," I said. "She's not black."

"What does she look like?" demanded Susan.

"I don't know." I said. "Blonde, like you."

"A lot like me?" she asked. "Is she tall?"

"Look, this is getting pretty complicated." Sweet Potato sharpened his back claws on my sofa. His front ones I had removed, but he was creative in the ways he devised to ruin the furniture and destroy the apartment. "I'd like it if we could stay friends," I told Susan.

"Just like that?" she said.

"Well, we had fun," I said. Sweet Potato pushed his head against my hand. "I had fun; didn't you?"

"I wasn't looking for fun," she said.

What was she looking for? I don't think she knew either. Change? Something different? I was looking for adventure to prove my life was not a lesbian version of middle-class monogamy. Now I had had an adventure and it was enough for a while.

"Then I'm sorry," I said, running my hand against the grain of Sweet Potato's hair until he bit me. I put him on the floor and held the receiver a little ways from my ear, waiting for Susan to hang up hard. She blew a police whistle into the phone instead and I dropped the receiver.

After a few minutes, the phone rang again.

"I'm sorry, baby," said Susan, "I just still think this could work."

Would you trade order and peace for passion and craziness?

Why did she want me? I don't know. Because now I didn't want her? Because I was committed to someone else? Because I was there? Susans are like that.

I was on the phone half the night before Susan conceded that our love was unilateral.

When I came to bed Em was waiting up for me, sitting with her knees tucked to her chest and filing her nails. She was rolled up like the angry fetuses anti-abortionists display in formaldehyde.

"I couldn't sleep," she said.

"That was the defense attorney we got for Bev," I offered again, hoping there would not be a fight.

"So I gathered," Em said flatly, "you and Naomi. Did you sleep with her?"

"No," I said, "of course not."

"You're full of shit," she said. "Don't lie to me."

"I wouldn't lie to you," I said.

"The hell you wouldn't. I heard you talking to her," said Em.

We went back and forth like that for quite a while, her accusing and me lying. Em finally got out of bed and put on her running clothes.

"I'm going for a walk," she said.

I looked at the alarm clock on our night stand. It was after midnight. To me, the city is a dangerous place filled with ugly people and ugly things like sharp knives hiding in the bottom of the dishwasher. I said, "I'm coming with you."

I pulled my dirty shorts out of the hamper by the dresser and followed her through the house putting on my clothes as I went and looking around for my running shoes. They were nearly new. I didn't run a lot. I had bought them to impress Em with my commitment to physical fitness when she first moved in. I found my shoes under the couch and put them on standing first on one foot then the other like a stork. "I'm coming with you," I said again.

I had in mind to protect her since it was so late at night. But Em was tall and strong and I was little and wimpy. She ran easy seven-minute miles and I wasn't even sure I could keep up. She was downstairs and out into the brick courtyard by the time I came out of the apartment. When I got to the street, it was empty. The sky was black with clouds spread out like cream over the stars and Em was nowhere in sight. It had rained all that evening and steam rose off the pavement from the puddles condensing in the heat. I ran as hard as I could down the middle of the street, along the route Em liked to take when she jogged in the mornings, until I couldn't catch my breath. I saw no one. The heat had made the air thick. It closed around me like a plastic bag and I stood bent over with my hands on my thighs under a street light waiting for my heart to idle back down again.

Then I walked back to our apartment in the fog, breathing through my mouth and jumping at every sound and shadow, afraid I would be raped. It was a strangely comforting thought. I would be raped. Em would see that I needed her then and wouldn't leave me. When I got home unmolested, Em was packing her things.

"What are you doing," I said.

But she wouldn't answer. I suppose it was self-evident.

She moved back in with her parents the next day and she sabotaged the toilet before she left so it ran constantly. The sound kept me up all night and I had to sleep at Naomi's until the plumber came and fixed it. Craziness is hard to keep isolated. It will metastasize all through ordinary lives.

X

I tried to reach Em every day from work, but she never returned my calls. One day I tried her and was amazed when she answered.

"Hi," I said. "Remember me?" I tried to sound off-hand.

Em hesitated. "Oh it's you, Ginny." She didn't sound happy to hear from me.

"Yes," I said. "It's me. How are you doing?"

"I'm fine."

"Me too," I said. "I'm fine." I lied.

"Great," she said. "That's great."

"Would you meet me for lunch sometime," I asked her finally. "Maybe tomorrow?" I asked.

She didn't answer.

"Next week then," I suggested.

"It's out of my way," Em said.

Her parents lived far from the business district in the Loop where I worked, on the Northwest side in a white ethnic neighborhood where you could get along just fine speaking nothing but Polish. Living in the most segregated city in the United States, there is an analogous ghetto for every ethnic group — Poles, Irish, Blacks, Indians, Chinese, you name it, contained by street names, the lines that people don't cross except to carry-out ethnic food. Here, the boundaries are called neighborhoods. It always seemed strange to me that people could live their lives in ten square blocks when my father had done everything he could to escape ghettoization.

A friend told me that her father was nineteen years old before he ever saw the lakefront. I could see Em living like that. With her butcher and the Polish bakery and her Catholic school parish within walking distance, how long, I wondered, would it take before she was completely reabsorbed by her ethnicity?

"I could come down on the El, I suppose," Em said after some thought.

"That's great," I said. I was elated. "That's really great." I was so happy all morning I didn't get any work done.

At noon, I went to wait for her in front of a fern bar on Wabash, looking in store windows until she arrived. We sat at a table by the window.

"How are your parents," I said. I entertained the belief that her mother genuinely liked me.

"They're happy I'm back home. My father missed me." She didn't look up from her menu.

I nodded. Her father was a silent, emotionless man.

"Dad asked how you were," she said.

"That was nice," I said. "Tell him I'm fine. I'm great." But I wasn't very convincing.

Em looked out the window. There was a blind man standing on the corner shaking a can of coins for rhythm and singing tunelessly with his head rolling around on his shoulders like Ray Charles. Every few minutes the El would go past above us and shake the street. At the tables, all the conversations got louder to drown out the roar of the train and then abruptly quieted down again when people realized the train had passed and they were still shouting. Then the El would come and everyone would shout again. I was listening to the conversations at the other tables, having none of my own to occupy me, and Em stared out the window, cool and moody, with her arms crossed under her chest.

"When are you coming home?" I asked her. I meant to my condo and it took her a while to understand that I thought someplace I owned was home to her.

She frowned a little. "Not just yet," she said. "Maybe after a while."

"I'm sorry," I said. I didn't know what "a while" meant.

Her menu lay open across her place. She folded it shut and watched the people in the street.

"I'm sorry," I said again.

"Yes," Em said, "I heard you."

The waitress came then and we ordered. Em told me she would still take care of my finances. I was surprised and thanked her.

"It's my job," she said. "Of course it's going to cost you."

I laughed, but she wasn't joking and I wondered if her rates had gone up.

"All right," I said.

"All right," she said. "I guess that's all."

She got up and walked out into the street leaving me with two lunches and a bill turned face down on a saucer. I watched her until she climbed the steps to the El platform. Then I ate both lunches and ordered dessert to console myself.

XI

Starr waved me over when I passed her desk.

"Come here, will ya?" She popped her gum and tossed my messages at me. "And this Coogan chick, will you please just call her back? She's driving me right up the fucking wall."

I took the messages. Five from Susan since I left for lunch, and one from a reporter regarding a company whose stock I followed. I dropped the message from the reporter in the trash. The rest were from Naomi.

"Sorry, Starr," I said.

She wrapped her gum around a finger. "It'd be okay but I'd just done my nails, you know? They were wet."

I didn't know but nodded anyway. Starr turned her attention back to the mirror on her desk and I headed back towards my office.

"You know, Ginny," she called after me, "why don't you just get a boyfriend."

I closed the door and called Susan. When I was a kid, I ate the food on my plate in descending order of preference to get it over with. Old habits die hard. I had an ax to grind with Susan; she was following me.

Riding the bus to work made me vulnerable to Susan's harassment. Fair is fair. I used her for sex and threw her over. I was willing to own that. It was okay that she filled up the tape on my answering machine so that no one else could leave any messages and haunted the street where I lived, but lately she had taken to riding my bus even though she lived across town.

Somehow, she would catch it before my stop and be riding it when I got on. Every day I would pay my dollar and walk down the rows of seats and there she'd be. She wouldn't say a thing, just smile at me like I was a stranger she might like to meet. Once when it rained, she dried the seat beside her as I walked down the aisle. I stood rather than sit there next to her. I was having trouble getting used to seeing her like that every day and I wanted to tell her to stop. We hadn't talked since the night Em left. I thought at this juncture maybe talking would help.

I called Susan's direct line and she answered in a voice she reserved for clients. It was sane and well-modulated, unlike anything I had heard on my phone machine recently.

"Susan?" I said, "hi," afraid that she would dissolve into her crazy self, but she didn't. She was the same as when I met her that first day at her office, very much in control.

"Why haven't you returned my calls? I've been calling you for weeks." She sounded as if I were the unstable one and she was only worried that I was okay.

"Since I see you every day, I don't really feel the need to call," I said.

"I don't think I know what you mean," Susan said.

I clenched my teeth. They were sore; I had been grinding them in my sleep. "Stop following me. Stop riding my bus."

"Was that you on the bus?" she said. "I wasn't sure."

"Stop riding my bus," I said again. This time I said it louder.

"I've moved North, Ginny. It *is* a free country," Susan explained with irrefutable logic. "You don't own the city buses."

"I know what you're doing," I said, but I really wasn't sure.

"You sound angry." Susan's voice had that calm-as-still-water-on-a-windless-day quality and it was making me very nervous. "Let's have lunch and talk," she said.

I had a horrible feeling that maybe she actually

hadn't been following me for the past two weeks. Then I started wondering who had been following me if it wasn't her.

Susan said, "Why don't you meet me tomorrow at Ramone's on Monroe; shall we say around one-ish?"

I agreed.

She was all business, but I was a basket case. Now I was hoping that the biggest problem I had was Susan.

When I called Naomi I was a little unglued, but I didn't mention lunch with Susan. The whole thing was just too embarrassing.

"Don't you get your messages?" Naomi said.

"Yeah," I said. "Does the U.S. Attorney ever put people under surveillance?"

"All the time," said Naomi. "What do you want to know about that for?"

"No reason," I said, but I kept bringing up the same question from different angles.

Naomi was losing patience with the conversation. "What exactly is wrong, Ginny? You sound like you're on speed."

"What if Susan isn't the one following me?" I asked.

"I don't know," Naomi laughed. "Who else have you fucked over lately?"

"Not funny," I said. "Do you think the Feds could be following me over that mail-tampering thing?"

Naomi said practically, "Why should they be following you? Why not just subpoena you?" She had a point and I felt a little better.

Naomi hadn't wanted anything special, just to kill time. The Feds were still looking hard for Mary Tally; otherwise she had nothing new to report.

"Are you planning to camp at my place tonight?" she said.

I told her I'd been thinking about it. I didn't have anywhere else to go. Since Em left, facing my apartment was hell, partially because she was the one who kept it clean. I only went there to shower in the mornings and feed Sweet Potato. Naomi wouldn't let me keep him at her place; she hated animals.

Ellen Borgia stopped by my office, full of news. She had met a man and we rejoiced in her good fortune. Ellen was careful not to rub my nose in it. She promised that I would meet one too someday, but reminded me that I was younger than she. Before she met this man, Ellen was loathe to admit that even she was starting to feel the urgency of her biological clock. Things had started going wrong with her body, as a punishment for not having babies, she believed. Just little things but nonetheless disturbing. Her periods had gotten nearly unbearable without prescription drugs. She held my gaze and I knew this admission evidenced for her the depth of our friendship. I hadn't thought that we were such pals, but I was touched by the emotion. It was nice to have one touching, human thing to think about that night when I reviewed my day. It kind of picked me up.

The other news from Ellen was that another white boy associate had announced that his wife was expecting. It was frightening. The white boys were procreating like flies at a picnic. Each one seemed to be having two and three children a year. I read once that before modern science, people believed that flies were spontaneously created. There is a word for that which I learned from the article: cryptogenic. People saw no connection between adult flies and maggots, believing maggots were the progeny of rotting food and excrement. One scientist, however, was sure that flies arose from maggots so he covered a jar of rotting food with a screen. The flies laid eggs on the screen because they could smell the food, and the maggots appeared on the screen far away from the food. I was beginning to believe that the offspring of the white boy associates really were cryptogenic because at the rate they were being produced no one could have had the energy to make them.

I shared that observation with Ellen and she laughed and squeezed my arm in a chummy summer camp kind of way. I wondered if she would have touched me like that if she'd known I was a lesbian. I wondered how she could not have known I was a lesbian.

Ellen giggled, which wasn't like her. "You know, everybody wants to be a white anglo saxon male. That, or kill one."

XII

That night Naomi poured me a glass of white wine and lit cigarette number ten or eleven. Her apartment always smelled like old smoke, but it was better than being alone. At home there were messages on my machine from Susan. They filled up the tape and when I erased them new ones appeared. I stopped erasing them. They said, "How can you be so unreasonable; I hate you." They said, "You're going to pay for using me; I could have made you so happy." They said, "I love you and now that she has gone, we can be together." But I had stopped listening to the promises and threats. I no longer answered the phone and only went home to change my clothes. I hid at Naomi's house eating her food and taking her sympathy such as it was. I wanted peace and order back in my life.

"You dumbshit," said Naomi, rehashing my misfortunes, "what possessed you to give Susan your home number? Why didn't you tell me you were going to sleep with her?"

"I didn't exactly plan it," I said and then wondered if I was telling the truth.

Naomi groaned. "Right," she said. "I forgot. With all our other problems you had to go do it with our defense attorney on a whim. She's crazy, you know."

I had to concede if single-minded pursuit is crazy then Susan had surely rounded the bend. When had she crossed the line? When she was buying me dinner? When she was driving me home? When she was fucking me with her hands against the door of her office? When she told me that she loved me in the dark? No. I liked all of those things. Craziness is in direct proportion to the annoyance it causes in other people's lives. Certainly society doesn't institutionalize people who have never bothered anyone.

You can adjust to anything after a while. Except for the new thing she'd started with the bus, I didn't let it bother me that Susan would not leave me alone. Since I had told her that I couldn't see her anymore, she had been following me to watch where I went at night. If I went home, I could see her car parked in the street from my balcony. After a while, when I drove to the grocery, I was surprised if I looked through my rearview mirror and she wasn't there.

"How could I have known beforehand?" I asked Naomi. "She was charming and has a responsible job. You said I would like her," I complained.

"Well, she is charming," Naomi admitted. Then she frowned. "But didn't I tell you the story of how she put a hole in a girl's wall when we were in law school?"

I didn't think it was a story I wanted to know. "No," I said. "You didn't mention that."

"Susan put her fist through this girl's wall at the dorm," said Naomi. "Broke her hand."

"Great. Do you think she would hurt me?" I said.

Naomi sipped her wine. "Naw. She'll just find someone else after a while. Susans are like hurricanes, you've got to wait for them to blow themselves out."

"Why'd she punch a hole in that woman's wall?" I asked.

Naomi laughed and drained her glass. "I don't know. Girl stopped sleeping with her, I guess." She poured herself another glass of wine and tipped the bottle in my direction. "You want some?" I passed her my glass and she filled it up to the lip.

Naomi can't sit still for long. She got busy walking in and out of the room emptying her ashtray and carrying food back and forth.

"Have you heard from Bev?" I was shouting so that Naomi could hear me in the kitchen or wherever she'd gone off to at that moment. Aside from missing Bev, I was starting to worry about her.

Naomi came back in the living room drying her

ashtray with a piece of paper towel. "No," she said. "With a little luck it won't matter if I do or not. The Feds still don't seem to have a clue that Bev and Kelsey were lovers; they've overlooked it completely with the separate apartments and the lease. They know Kelsey was a lesbian but they're still focused on the Boston girl, Mary Tally, as the love interest. They still can't find her. Her roommate at the apartment where she was living says she just moved out with no forwarding address. The police think maybe she was in Chicago the night Kelsey was killed. People at her office confirm she was there in Boston all day that Wednesday. Her time card said she punched out at five-oh-five Wednesday night. She could have gotten to Chicago easily in time to kill Kelsey on a six o'clock flight out of Logan. The coroner's report says Kelsey died sometime after nine pm and before two am. The last flight to Boston leaves O'Hare at eight-twenty-five and there's nothing out of Midway Airport on the southside so that's out of the question. But the first flight in the morning gets in at nine-ten and we know that Mary punched in late at ten-thirty on Thursday morning." Naomi took her lighter from the coffee table and lit another cigarette.

"Why did they think Mary Tally was here, besides being late for work the next day?" I asked. There seemed to be too many pieces in this puzzle.

"The bartender saw a black woman in a fashion headwrap in the bar with Kelsey the night she died. At least she thought she was black, maybe Latino," said Naomi. "Didn't I tell you?"

She hadn't told me. "Is Mary Tally black?" I

asked. I was ready to be sure that Kelsey was a racist as well as an opportunist and was deflated that it looked now like she was just an opportunist.

Naomi laughed, probably reading my mind. "I think old Kelsey liked black women, Ginny. Are you surprised?"

I was. I was surprised, but I pretended I wasn't. After that I didn't have much to say. This was a new twist and I needed to think about it. I ran my finger around and around the lip of my wine glass until it made a ringing noise. Naomi smoked.

Kelsey's murder had been starting to look like a non-event. Mary Tally was on the lam, Kelsey and Nealy were dead, and the Feds had no one to bring to trial. The money they had stolen was chump change compared to their other cases. The Feds were on a budget and the hot topic was drug money. From Halligan's, the DA's, point of view, the case might have been dead in the water. With the only lead in Boston and the Feds pulling out, he wasn't about to spend his precious budget putting cops on a plane to stake out some apartment in Boston to find Mary Tally. And the Boston cops had their own fish to fry. They would barely be willing to arrest Mary Tally if she walked into city hall to pay her parking tickets.

"You know, Ginny, I'm sorry you got us into this," Naomi said. I felt like shit all over again then, even though most of our problems weren't my fault. The scam with the mail had opened a can of worms. That's what Naomi was getting at.

"Me too. I lost a good friend, Naomi." I said it as a minor point in my defense. I hadn't talked to Bev since she kicked me out of her apartment. She wouldn't return my calls at work and her answering machine was on all the time. I took it as a hint.

Naomi tapped a long trail of ash into an ashtray and put her cigarette down on the side. The smoke rolled past her face like a veil. "Hey. She was my friend too," Naomi said a little too easily. "The bad news is I'm not sure anymore that this will blow over."

Naomi exhaled, letting the smoke drift out through her nose. "Halligan needs to find an in-town killer to get Jose Alvarez and those politicos at Gay and Lesbian Task Force off his back, but he's running out of suspects. They're all turning up dead." Naomi laughed. Then she said: "I know that's not funny, but it's true."

"What about Mary Tally," I said. "She's not dead."

Naomi shook her head. "We don't know that. I'm worried Halligan is going to start looking for a killer hard enough to find out that Bev and Kelsey were lovers. He hasn't focused on her living arrangements and that's what's kept Bev safe so far, but the police have just got to ask enough people long enough to find out."

I didn't see it. "Who's he going to ask?" I said.

"Neighbors with suspicions. Anybody." Naomi threw up her hands. "I don't know, but somebody has got to know that Bev is a dyke. Hell, he just has to interrogate Bev again and ask the right questions. If he does, we're back to where we were with some serious problems to take care of."

I took a drink of my wine; it was helping my brain to unkink. I needed that to sleep at nights. "This is not great," I said.

"No, we need some more suspects to entertain the police." Naomi ran her fingers through the front of her hair and sighed. "What we need is to turn up Mary Tally. That would help a lot."

I didn't know whether she was hinting or just complaining. "So, do you think Mary Tally killed Kelsey?" I really wanted to know.

Naomi recrossed her legs. "At this point the question is academic. I suppose a lot of people could have done it. The police are still looking in pawn shops for a murder-robbery angle. They picked up some punk trying to pawn Kelsey's college ring in Uptown. First he claimed someone had given him the ring. Then he said Kelsey was already dead when he took it off her. He didn't have any of the other stuff. People she worked with said she wore a Rolex watch." Naomi thought for a while. "I think I remember the Rolex."

I remembered the Rolex. I wasn't surprised anymore when I saw them on the arms of people I knew, but I was socialized to notice. Your watch was a sign of rank, signaling as elaborately as anything Marlin Perkins ever talked about on *Wild Kingdom*. It told people you were in the game without you even opening your mouth to brag, that you could drop a bundle on a fashion accessory that worked no better than a drugstore Timex. Of course, nobody I knew bought those power watches for list price. That's what the discount jewelers out in the northwest suburbs are for. With what I knew about Kelsey's finances, I didn't imagine she was any different.

My own watch had cost more than I spent on groceries in six months and had no numbers on its face so it was hell to tell what time it was. I'd bought it before Em cut up my credit cards. But it suddenly looked cheesy to me and I put it in the pocket of my jeans. What I didn't want was more similarities to Kelsey.

That the Rolex hadn't turned up yet made me wonder. I guess it made the police wonder too because they charged the punk with robbery instead of murder. "I wonder who killed her?" It was a rhetorical question.

"Who knows who?" Naomi shrugged. "Bev could have done it for that matter. You weren't with her that night until eleven-thirty and Kelsey could have been shot before that. She had the oldest motive in the world."

"That's pretty stupid," I said, "particularly since I just got caught cheating and I'm still here to talk about it."

Naomi rolled her eyes. "Don't get touchy, Ginny," she said, "I was just making a point. Anyone could have killed Kelsey for any reason. There are three million people in this city living like rats in a cage and people get themselves killed all the time. If the police stop caring who killed Kelsey, I sure as hell am not going to worry about it any more. But for now, we need some more people for the cops to suspect or you and me could be in some deep shit PDQ. It would be nice if they could find this Mary Tally."

Naomi as usual had a tenable point. Mary Tally was definitely a front runner. But, personally, I was having some nagging doubts, embarrassingly, about Bev and what she was doing before she met me the night Kelsey got killed. It was starting to bother me that she'd tried to give me a gun the day after the murder and I didn't much like to be bothered in that way.

For me, there were a lot of unanswered questions and the loose ends to Kelsey's murder were keeping me up nights — that, or it was Naomi's sofa bed. For example: If Kelsey was rich from embezzling why did she look poor in her accounts and why did she need to use Bev to pay her mortgage? If her partners killed her why did they do such a messy job? Where was Mary Tally? I had a funny feeling she wasn't dead. It seemed to me like she might be the key to all of this and from Naomi's description of things, the police just weren't looking hard enough for her.

That night, when the sofa bed had given me a backache I couldn't sleep through, I decided to do some looking for Mary Tally on my own. I made a note in my daytimer to check my frequent flier miles to see if I could get to Boston for free.

XIII

Lunch with Susan turned out to be quite a production. I had never been to Ramone's and when I walked in I knew why. My idea of lunch is some greasy spoon under the El tracks or Popeye's Fried Chicken where I'm not ashamed to say I eat. I steal off every once in a while to the Popeye's off Dearborn in the Loop to get my two-piece dinner with a biscuit and Cajun rice, sitting with the other well-heeled grease addicts on the stools by the window with a premium view of the dumpsters in the alley. I eat fast and regret my selection for the rest of the day, popping Rolaids like candy now that the Irishman has made my stomach a cantankerous organ.

If I want to go to a nice lunch, it's that fern bar where I took Em, but that's about as nice as it gets. Ramone's was in a different league and I was starting to get the message, so was Susan in a lot of ways. It wasn't just for the prices, although those helped. It was the private elevator from the street level down to a dining room where everyone was dressed like a maitre d'.

Susan was waiting for me in one of her Barbara Stanwyck power suits. She took my hand with a firm grip, and managed to successfully select the actual maitre d', who was standing behind a little podium, from among the collection of about a million ordinary waiters. If I'd been her date, I would have been impressed. She walked close behind one of our waiters to the table as if she ate there a lot. Maybe she did — she had managed to get a booth in a dark corner which I took to be something of a coup. The waiter pulled the table out and Susan watched while I slid in first. The waiters, of which there were at least three, hovered and fawned. Susan leaned towards the pretty-boy taking the orders as if they were girlfriends.

She listened to the specials and ordered for me without asking what I wanted. I thought I could use a beer, but Susan had ordered a bottle of California Chardonnay before I could open my mouth. I was so angry I couldn't speak. That was fine, as Susan had clearly planned to do the talking. She started with pleasantries, leaning too close and patting my hand so often that she was almost stroking it.

"So how are you doing?" she said, as the waiter brought around the wine. "I feel like we haven't really talked in a while."

The waiter opened the bottle and put the cork down by her place. Then he stood at attention while Susan rolled the wine around in her glass and her mouth for a while. He filled her glass and mine and then went away.

"I've really missed you," Susan went on, "but I guess I've said that already."

I wondered if the waitstaff standing at her elbow had heard it too, but Susan ignored them. They, for their part, pretended there was nothing more interesting than the empty space in front of their noses, which they studied politely and with their eyes fixed. Ramone's was a classy place.

This was my cue to say that I had missed her too, but I didn't. I gave the water glass my undivided attention which resulted in it being refilled several times.

Susan marshalled her forces for another assault. "It really hurt me that you sounded so angry on the phone," she said. "I've been worried about you."

I bent over my salad which was quite good, but it didn't improve my mood. "I've been fine," I said.

Susan wiped Ramone's special shrimp dressing off her chin before one of our waiters could do it for her and arranged her napkin back over her thigh. She laid her fork and knife on the side of her plate and folded her hands. I blinked and her salad plate had vanished.

Susan said, "You haven't been staying at home."

She said it like she knew where I was staying

and like she had a grave personal interest in the sleeping arrangements at Naomi's. I didn't answer.

The entree came, but I was too angry to eat. Just her sitting there made me angry. I felt manipulated, into bed, into lunch, into feeling as if she were sane and that I might be crazy and a little immature. I resented it a lot.

"You're not staying at your apartment," Susan said again.

"No, I'm not," I said. "Stop following me."

Susan, of course, ignored the imperative. "You know I could love you, Ginny," she said.

This is where I was supposed to realize that, having touched her genitals, I loved her too.

She paused and sighed, looking around the dining room. "I don't understand you, Ginny," she said as if to indicate this lifestyle could be ours if I'd only play nice.

"I'd like you to stop following me," I said. "That's all I want. Is that so hard to understand?"

Susan put her fork down hard and sulked. "I do everything I can to make things nice for you and you don't appreciate it."

"Well," I started, but as a matter of fact, I didn't.

"I'm not following you," continued Susan. "Sometimes I happen through your neighborhood. There's no law against that."

"No. But stop it," I said, "and we will get along better. While you're at it, if we should find ourselves in the same restaurant, which I doubt, don't ever order for me again."

"You don't like your food?" Susan looked heartbroken.

"That's not the point," I said. "I'd just like to choose it myself."

"I brought you here to lunch," said Susan, "it seems to me whether you like your food or not is exactly the point. I wouldn't have brought you here if I didn't think you'd like it."

"Has anyone ever told you you're kind of a control freak?" I asked her. It was the wrong thing to say.

"Fine," she said. "I can see you're not interested in a constructive dialogue."

She wiped her mouth, balled up her napkin and threw it at me. Then she slid her thick legs out of the booth.

"Where are you going?" I asked.

Susan smoothed her skirt. "To the john," she said.

I couldn't argue with that, but I did wonder what the john looked like here. I suspected it was the kind of place where you had to buy your hand towel from an old black woman and I resolved to hold my business until I got back to Whytebread where the restrooms were free.

My fish was actually delicious. I ate it with much more relish now that Susan was not there to watch me, and soaked up all the free ambiance when I had finished the last of it.

Susan had been gone for ten minutes and I started to worry. One of our waiters asked if he could take my plate, and made some dessert suggestions which I declined. Then, the pretty one came around with a little book which I suspected held the check.

"Your friend said she had to go but that you

116

would take care of this. Thank you so much," he said through thin, pursed lips. "Please do come again."

"Oh no," I said. "Thank you."

Em had cut up all of my personal credit cards, but I still had my corporate card from Whytebread. I just put the plastic in the book. I didn't even want to look at the bill. I figured I'd just had better than a hundred-dollar lunch, but at least I had some closure.

Susan stopped riding my bus and if she still followed me in her car, she got more discreet after that.

I started sleeping at home instead of Naomi's. My bed was better than Naomi's sleeper sofa, but it felt huge and empty without Em in it. Em sleeps stretched out unless she's angry, and she tosses, taking up much more than her share of the bed. I had learned to sleep curled up requiring very little room. Now with her gone, I had forgotten how to fill the space. It's funny the things you notice when people leave. Sweet Potato had taken to sleeping on Em's side but it wasn't the same.

I decided to go to Boston over the weekend with my mileage awards. I hate to fly. At takeoff and landing I feel especially close to death since I read that they are the most dangerous times. But, I needed to do something and going to Boston was something.

I decided to stop by Bev's before I went. I can't explain why. Maybe to prove to myself that she could not have killed Kelsey so that I could cross her off my list of suspects. Maybe I wanted to prove to her that I was her friend.

Bev and I were connected by race and class and experience in a way I was not connected to too many other people in a city segregated on all of those fronts. Her friendship was in some respects irreplaceable and I was feeling its loss. I didn't know as many middle-class black lesbians as I would have liked. Bev could understand and share the breadth of my experience without my having to explain it, or translate it as I did for Em to a more familiar context. I did not have to paint for her the backdrop of my American history. Bev understood how hard it is to know that there is nothing happier than little black girls coming from the beauty parlor or nothing sadder than little black girls in the rain.

So, I invited myself to Bev's apartment on Thursday night. My flight to Boston was Friday after work. Bev seemed a little cool, but she let me in and I had a seat. I thought she was maybe ready to make up too.

"Do you want a beer?" she asked.

They were left over from the housewarming and she was trying to get rid of them. The housewarming seemed like years ago and the apartment seemed sadder than the last time I was there, darker, more closed off. Bev was packing her things. There were boxes everywhere and the blinds were shut.

"Yeah," I said. "I'd drink a beer." I laughed. "I'll always drink a beer."

She motioned for me to help myself. The bottles were in a stack in the vegetable crisper at the bottom of her refrigerator and there was a can opener stuck with a magnet on the side of the ice box.

I sat down on the couch and put my beer glass down on her coffee table. "What are you doing?" I asked.

Bev slid a coaster under my glass. "Packing."

"That's what it looks like," I said.

She kept packing. I could tell it was getting her down. She said, "Kelsey's family is going to sell this place. They gave me the option of staying until my lease is up, with people walking through all the time, or moving out at the end of the month."

"I'm sorry," I said. "That's really hard."

She shook her head. "I don't want to stay here anymore."

I asked her where she would go and offered my apartment again. "Em's left me," I said. "I've got plenty of room."

Bev was shocked. She looked sadder than I was about it. "What happened?"

"We grew apart," I said and truly that is what I thought had happened. "Now I've got plenty of space and you're welcome."

Bev said she'd taken a little studio downtown for a while and was putting her things in storage. "You know I had to sit at Kelsey's funeral like I was less than an acquaintance, someone who rented a downstairs apartment. Kelsey's mother told me how nice she thought it was that a tenant would take time off work to come."

I didn't know what to say; nothing seemed like enough.

"I didn't even have some private time to say goodbye," said Bev. She didn't say anything else and I didn't like the silence.

"I'm going to Boston to find that girl," I said.

Bev perked up a little and I rattled along. "Naomi got the girl's address from a friend at the U.S. Attorney. She's got a lot of connections there." I didn't tell her we'd read Kelsey's mail. "I can't give you the address. Naomi didn't even want to give it to me and please, don't tell her I'm going out there."

"I don't want to know where that woman is," said Bev flatly. Her voice had an ugly note to it that I'd not heard before. "I'm sure she killed Kelsey." Then she started to cry again.

I handed her a Kleenex from a big wad I had in my purse. I always carried them in case a bus seat is wet or something. After a while Bev pulled herself together.

"What flights will you be on, honey?" she asked. "And where are you staying so I won't worry."

It was nice to have someone concerned about me now that Em had taken off. With Bev calling me "honey" again I figured things were on the mend. I gave her my flight numbers and the number of the hotel. I agreed that if something came up, I would call her and she would call the police.

The head on my beer had gone away but the beer was still good and cold. "You know," I said, "I was just trying to help when I suggested that lawyer."

"Forget about it, honey," Bev said.

I asked her to feed Sweet Potato while I was gone. She promised she would. I sat back on the couch while Bev packed up her things and I treated myself to another beer since the first one was so good.

XIV

I told Starr I had to get my teeth cleaned on Friday and left at 2:30 pm to catch the 4:30 pm flight to Boston from O'Hare. I put a pair of jeans and some underwear in my briefcase along with a tee shirt and my toothbrush, and wore sneakers with my suit to the airport.

On my way out to the Kennedy Expressway, I had the cab drop me at Gloria's Place where Kelsey was killed to talk to the bartender about Mary Tally. I had no idea how I would know her if I found her.

Gloria's is a big place with two bars and a

good-sized dance floor. Space is a lot of its appeal. Women's bars are generally dingy little holes that don't see much daylight. Gloria's is different. The inside is deco, all glass and chrome. There is a high tech DJ booth in the center of the dance floor. Gloria's belongs to a new generation of women's glamour bars where being underdressed on a Saturday night is a possibility.

I walked in past the big dyke who watches the door. It was five o'clock and there was no one in the place but me and the bartender. She was midwestern nondescript with thin brown hair cut in a way that didn't flatter her, but she was friendly enough. Like all women who tend bar, she thought she was hot.

"What can I get you?" she asked.

I sat myself on a stool in the center of the bar and watched my reflection in the mirror behind her.

"Whatever's on tap," I said. "Light beer." I patted my stomach where some paunch was starting.

"Didn't you used to come in here with a woman named Kathy?" The bartender washed dishes behind the bar while she made conversation.

That was years ago. "Yeah. Do I know you?" I said.

She shook her head. "No. I just remember you, that's all." She brought another beer over and filled my glass from the bottle. "It's on me," she said.

I watched myself thank her in the mirror. I was looking pretty good these days.

"Do you have a name?" I asked.

She leaned forward with her hands on the bar and wet her lips. "That's a pretty corny line, but my name's Anne with an e on the end."

"It wasn't a line." I finished my beer. "That was genuine curiosity. Tell you what," I said, "were you working the night that girl got killed in the alley?"

She tossed her head. Her hair was cut in one of those schoolboy-looking styles, long on the top and shaved underneath. "Why do you want to know?"

"More curiosity," I said. "I like your hair."

She tossed her head again, flattered. "Really?" she said. "I just changed it."

"It looks good," I lied, and she topped off my glass with more free beer. "Were you working?"

"Yeah. I was working," she said. "The police freaked everybody out. All the women practically ran out of here when they showed up."

I smiled. "But you talked to the police, right?"

"Oh right," she said. "That Kelsey was a regular. I mean I would know her to see her. Like you."

"I thought I was special."

"You know what I mean," she said, but she didn't blush.

"So what happened?" I took a long drink of my free beer.

The bartender took a breath. "I found her in the back when I took out the trash at closing and called the police. They were nice, the police, and I was pretty shaky."

"I can understand that," I said.

She smiled more weakly this time, remembering what had happened. "You bet. Two women officers came in to ask questions. They're regulars too when they're off duty."

"Didn't you hear anything, a shot?" I asked.

The bartender shrugged. "It was Women of Color Wednesday. The music was loud and people were dancing. The police said she could have been shot anytime from nine pm to two am. In this neighborhood you hear things all the time. I'm no detective," she added.

"Who do you think did it?" I asked.

She shrugged again. She was tired of the topic, but twenty questions was something to do. "I told them about a black woman in a scarf who came in here and sat with that Kelsey. She was eyeing the girls all right, but that's the only one she talked to all night. They left together. I thought it was a pickup. End of story."

"Did Kelsey talk to you?" I asked.

The bartender dried a glass and took out a bottle of beer for herself. "Sure. Everybody talks to me."

"How did she seem, Kelsey, I mean?"

The bartender tossed her head some more and shrugged. "I don't know. How does anybody seem? What's your interest, really."

"Curiosity," I said, "honest. What did the black woman look like?"

The bartender shook her head. She said that it was dark and the woman wore shades.

"Didn't you think it was weird for her to be wearing shades at night?" I asked.

"The police asked that, but it takes all kinds. I just serve drinks," she said. "Listen, I get off work at six. Why don't you hang around."

"I'd like to really, but I've got a plane to catch." I said, "Keep my seat warm, will you?"

"I'll do that." The bartender threw me a wink on my way out the door.

I flagged another cab to the airport.

The plane trip was uneventful, but the flight took

off two hours late. A woman in front of me looked like a Latina version of a Nagel print with black, black hair pulled back off her face in a short ponytail. Her hair wasn't long enough for a ponytail. It was blunt-cut well above her shoulders, which were like a swimmer's, wide enough to land an Air Force jet, but it was clear she knew that the style showed her face to its best advantage.

It was a face I preferred strongly to the book I was reading and I was disappointed that her seat was so far in front of mine that it prevented me from staring. She was tall and when she stretched to put her luggage in the overhead, there was a thin, brown line of waist between her biker jacket and her blue jeans. When she bent to pick up the second piece, the cheeks of her ass showed through the jeans like nice cleavage. I flattered myself that she was watching me too and wondered briefly if the seat next to her was empty. It wasn't, but I had peace of mind that the plane would not fall out of the sky today because surely a benevolent New Testament God wouldn't take such a creature out of this world. We didn't get to Logan until ten o'clock Boston time. I'd had three beers on the plane: one on the ground and two in the air and I was beat.

I took a cab to the Marriot, ordered room service and took a long hot bath. I tried Bev's number, but got her machine. I left a message.

The next day, Saturday, I got up at nine and bought a street map from the information booth by the front desk. Mary Tally's apartment, it turned out, wasn't in Boston proper, but in a place called Brighton. I caught a cab in front of the hotel to the address we got from Mary Tally's letters. It wasn't the greatest neighborhood. It was bad by blocks, but it didn't raise my blood pressure too much.

I was hoping Mary Tally had a roommate I could talk to or maybe a friendly neighbor willing to put her business in the street. The building was a walk-up with so many flights of stairs that I hoped I hadn't come for nothing. I knocked, and a woman with a pierced nose and a shaved head answered. I told her my name was Bev Johnson and I was looking for Mary Tally.

"She's not here." The Nose Ring started to close the door. She looked like a seventeen-year-old male marine recruit.

"Does your mother know you did that to your hair?" I asked.

She didn't crack a smile and I put the toe of my sneaker in the door just in case. "Look," I said, "I know the police are looking for Mary, but I'm not with the police."

She looked like she didn't believe me for a minute.

"Honest," I said. "I rented an apartment from Kelsey and I have something she said Mary should have if anything happened to her."

I hoped the story didn't sound too cryptic. I was making it up as I went along, but the Nose Ring didn't close the door.

"What have you got?" she asked.

"I don't have it with me," I improvised. "Besides, how do I know you'll give it to Mary and not the police?"

"I don't talk to the police, that's why," she announced. "They are the patriarchy."

"Yeah?" I said. "That's a big word. Why don't you

take my number. If Mary turns up, please tell her I'm looking for her. It's important. Kelsey was my good friend and I promised her I'd give this package to Mary, but I'll only be in town until Sunday afternoon."

She took the number and yawned without covering her mouth, but I was pretty sure I had her on the hook.

"If I see Mary, I'll tell her," she said.

"I like the nose ring," I told her but the conversation was clearly over.

I moved my foot out of the way just in time to avoid having it closed in the door. Then I had to walk five blocks waving my arms before I got a cab back to the hotel. When I got back to my room, the message light was flashing on my phone. The desk said I was supposed to meet a friend at noon in front of the columns at Quincy Market. That was all there was to the message and I figured it had to be from Mary Tally.

I tried again to call Bev but she was out. I left another message on her machine and then I looked at my watch. It said eleven o'clock. I decided to walk it.

Quincy Market is on Congress Street. The man at the desk told me I couldn't miss it. He was right. Quincy Market looks like Boston's answer to Pier 39 or Ghiradelli Square. It is a low-rise watertower if you use Chicago as a point of reference, with jugglers and puppet shows and guys with long hair playing "Leaving on a Jet Plane" on their guitars for spare change.

It is wall-to-wall people at noon on Saturday and I could understand why someone who didn't want to be found might agree to meet there; it was a perfect place to get lost in a crowd. I had no idea how she would find me but I leaned on a gray concrete column and waited. A guy with a life-sized hand puppet, "Pirate Jack," shouted friendly witticisms at people in the crowd. It was a pretty good puppet show and I didn't mind the wait.

At exactly noon, someone tapped me on the shoulder. She wore a black leather mini with a zipper up the front, a lace camisole and a biker jacket. She had that honey-brown hair ala Tina Turner that seems to be enjoying a resurgence on black women. It was tied up in a cloth band. I thought that this was not the outfit I would pick if I were incognito, but then I noticed at least five other women around in roughly the same costume.

"You Beverly Johnson?" she said.

"Yeah." I hadn't figured out what I was going to do yet. "Are you Mary Tally?" I asked.

She put her hand on her hip. "Maybe," she said. "Let's walk, okay?"

"All right," I said.

We walked. Mary Tally had a walk that could stop traffic on the turnpike.

"How old are you?" I said. She looked fifteen.

She smiled. "Old enough. Twenty-three. How old are you?"

"I'm twenty-seven," I said.

"You don't look it."

"Thanks," I said.

"Sure. So what have you got for me?"

"Are you Mary Tally?" I asked her again.

"Yeah," she said. "What have you got?"

"How can I be sure?" I asked. "Show me something to prove it."

She hesitated for a minute then pulled a wallet from the pocket of her jacket. She took a driver's license out and handed it to me. There was a picture of her in a Boston University sweatshirt and a headband. The name on the license was Mary E. Tally. I handed it back to her and she put it in her wallet. "Satisfied?" she asked.

I nodded. "Yeah." I was satisfied. "Did you go to BU?"

"I dropped out," she said. "So what you got for me?"

I took an envelope from my purse. It was a prop; there was nothing in it.

Mary Tally reached for it.

"Not here," I said. "Someplace more private."

She shrugged and pointed to a restaurant off the square. "Let's eat then. You pay."

We got a table upstairs. It wasn't the best one they had and I didn't know if it was because we were two women or two blacks, but I wasn't in the mood to make waves. Mary had demanded the smoking section before I could stop her. When we sat down she lit up with a lot of attitude. Mary smoked menthols. She offered me one.

"No thanks," I said. "I don't smoke."

"Good for you," she said. "I'm trying to quit. I got asthma."

The restaurant was nearly empty and the waitress paid us a lot of attention. She looked like a poster child for the Seven Sisters. Mary ordered dessert and a decaf espresso. I had lunch, a hamburger and some beer.

Mary sat across from me with one leg tucked up under the other and her cigarette tucked in the corner of her mouth like the tough girl I didn't really take her for. Her cigarette bobbed up and down as she moved her lips.

"Now, what have you got for me?" she asked again.

I handed her the envelope. She was noticeably pissed when there was nothing in it.

"What the fuck is this?" she said.

"Look," I said, "I'm sorry. I'm not Beverly Johnson, but I'm a friend." It must have sounded lame.

Mary Tally may have looked like she'd been born yesterday, but she wasn't. "What exactly do you want?" she said. I could see she was checking out her exit strategies.

"I want to find out who killed Kelsey," I told Mary. "Seems to me, the way you loved her, you'd want to find that out too."

Mary Tally relaxed. Something I had said struck her really funny. She put her cigarette down and threw her head back so she could laugh better. She laughed from her chest which was round and firm. I would have found the laugh engaging if she hadn't been laughing at me. "Whoever you are, you're misinformed, but clearly you're harmless and you're surely not the police." She took a drink of her coffee and grimaced. "I don't know whether to set you straight or let you stay this stupid."

"Why don't you set me straight." Mary was starting to piss me off.

"All right," she said. She had sized me up from my Cole Haan loafers to my college signet ring. She had a chip on her shoulder for people like me and she wanted to make sure I knew she was at least as smart as I was, even if she didn't have a diploma. "What do you want to know?"

I had about a million questions and they started with why Kelsey was so broke if she was embezzling all that cash and ended with who had killed Kelsey. In between, I wanted to know about her partners and where Bev came in.

Mary ordered another espresso. "Kelsey taught me how to drink these," she remarked in a way that made me think that Kelsey might not have been so bad. "Let me tell you a story."

She put out her cigarette and took her time.

Mary had met Kelsey at a company Christmas Party when Kelsey was supervising an audit in the Boston division. Mary said that she could have spotted Kelsey a mile away with her wide-stepping dyke swagger and she figured Kelsey knew her story too. Kelsey got drunk and backed her into a corner at the party. Afterward, whenever Kelsey came into town, she started hanging around the accounting department where Mary worked.

"She wouldn't go away until I went to dinner with her. She took me to a fancy place in the city near her hotel. Yeah." Mary smiled to herself about the particulars. "We had some laughs. Kelsey was —" My beer got two degrees warmer while Mary sifted through her vocabulary for the right descriptor. She said finally, "Kelsey was sweet." The way she said it, I knew exactly what she meant.

"Kelsey was sweet, but, you know, a little simple; she wanted me to quit my job and come live with her in Chicago, not work, just be her wife." Mary thumped her chest. "Look at me, girlfriend, I couldn't be anybody's wife. Now, could I?"

I admitted she had a point, but so far Mary hadn't told me one single thing of use and my patience was wearing out. "Okay," I said, "so sweet Kelsey took you to dinner and tried to make an honest woman out of you. Can we speed it up?"

I had hurt her feelings. "If you'd let me talk, I'd tell you what you want to know." Mary articulated every word. When she finished telling me off she crossed her arms and was sullen. "I was getting to it." The pout was becoming; kind of a Lolita thing.

I said I was sorry and she went on stubbornly in her weaving, rambling, remembering way, picking up color and momentum as she went.

"I couldn't be anybody's cooking, cleaning wife and I don't care if she said we'd get a maid because you now you've got to clean up before they come. I can't be having those strings and demands on me. Kelsey was sweet, but she was nothing but strings."

Mary told me her real lover was a video artist who understood about freedom and didn't care about monogamy.

"Kelsey didn't understand at all and the more she tried to hold me, the more I had to get away. She was jealous and she wanted me where she could watch me. She tried to buy me things to get me to want to live with her." Mary shrugged. "The last thing she bought was that house and from the minute she got it she was all the time after me and after me to move in with her. She thought she could buy me with all her money." Remembering seemed to suddenly make her sad.

"And it wasn't fun anymore?" I asked.

Mary lit another cigarette and blew the smoke out. "No," she said. "It wasn't fun. That was when I got the idea to make some money of my own. I'd worked for the company since I was nineteen and I was tired of seeing people right out of college with no more brains in their heads than that —" Mary snapped her fingers, "— get promoted over me. Just like that they were promoted, and people like Kelsey too. I was still a clerk like when I started and I was tired of it."

I told her I could understand and she looked at me as if she wanted to believe it was true.

Mary Tally had worked for Jim Nealy, the head accountant in Boston, for a long time. She knew he liked to bet on the ponies. Nealy had had his hand in the till for years, small potatoes, but it added up. He knew how to cover his tracks and work the system so nobody noticed where accounts didn't balance here and there. Mary knew her way around Nealy. She knew that Nealy, not wanting to expose his own embezzlement, would look the other way if he noticed hers, but she didn't know the system beyond her department and she needed someone outside accounting to cover her tracks. Kelsey was responsible for the audits and accounts of all the divisions in the Northeast. She was proud of her job and she bragged about it to Mary. When Mary showed an interest, Kelsey explained the checks and balances of the whole accounting system to her and Mary was a very quick study.

"I told her if she wanted me to come and live with her, she'd have to help us make a lot of money fast and then we could go away, just the two of us. The first time I brought it up, she said no right away. She said she had a responsibility to the company."

"What made her change her mind?" I asked, "besides you?"

Mary crossed her legs and smiled. I could see that flattery was going to get me everywhere. "Kelsey was up for a promotion and she didn't get it. She was mad. She said they passed over her because she was a woman. She thought they had found out she was a dyke."

"And she said she'd help you then?"

"Kelsey liked the idea all right," Mary said, "but she was scared we'd get caught. I told her if anybody got wind of it, Nealy would be the first one they'd suspect and we would leave before anybody suspected her."

I didn't have a real clear understanding of the particulars of Mary's swindle. I'm a securities analyst, not a bookkeeper, but the way she talked I got the picture that she had thought it out very well from the start. Mary Tally might not have had a Ph.D, but she had a mind with knife edges and I was having a tough time keeping up. Em could probably have explained it to me in perfect clarity, but after our lunch that day, the only communications I'd gotten from Em were advices that she'd paid herself a monthly fee out of my accounts.

As near as I could piece together, the swindle went like this: Mary wrote out a purchase order for office supplies, something small, costing a nominal amount of money that would not be questioned. She submitted it, and the purchase order wound its way through the usual channels getting signed-off on by whoever needed to do it. Who had the final approval, I don't know. It really didn't matter. The purchase order came back to Mary in the accounting department because she cut the checks. When her purchase orders came back, she'd change the amounts and initial the change with her supervisor, Nealy's initials. Then, she'd get the check cut and pocket the money.

Mary needed Kelsey or someone like her because a copy of the purchase order she got back went to audit. That copy would not have been changed; it would read for the original party and the original amount requested. Kelsey controlled audit and she had access to that paper trail. She pulled the copies and changed them so that the audit records matched the accounting records. That way when the staff checked accounting there were no flats. It sounded very slick.

I won't tell you that Mary Tally's scheme was ethical. But when I looked at her I saw myself in different circumstances. I saw a woman with some brains in a country where women are valued for our bodies. I saw a black face where blackness is valued not at all. I could not judge her.

We had come from different places to arrive in

this moment at the same place and with her story she was telling me the Secret. Letting me in on something, in case I didn't know it already, so it didn't jump up and bite me in my college-educated ass someday when I was unprepared. And she smiled a little when she saw I took her meaning, the way people smile at a small town scandal.

In the back of my mind, along with a fear of the dark I thought I'd outgrown, there was her smile and the words of Ralph Ellison's nightmare, "To whom it may concern: Keep this black boy running." And the sound of it was the sound of my own voice, cracked and whispering in the back of my head, coming now from the mouth of someone else. The Secret was: the game is rigged and even when you black folks think you're winning, you are not — that she and I, as different as we might seem to one another, were the same in the final analysis to the people who had control of the prizes. The Secret was that as long as we both were black, some bastard I could buy and sell would still feel justified in calling me a name in the street, some woman might not dance with me because she didn't like the texture of my hair, and there were still places where I couldn't play golf.

I smiled back at her larceny because in that moment I loved her for her willingness to share with me the punch line to the running joke of my life, knowing it had not been taught to me at my private schools and my fancy universities, suspecting that my parents fruitlessly pulling at the leather of their own bootstraps had tried to shield me from it in the hope that it might not be true.

Mary was saying, "If the Game is rigged, you have to cheat." While I was still looking for my own solution to the problem, I could not condemn her for hers.

I asked her if she'd thought the scam up by herself.

"It was my idea. But my girlfriend helped," she said as an afterthought. Mary was vain about her intelligence. She didn't want you to think she was just a pretty face.

"Your girlfriend, Kelsey?" I was surprised. I had thought Kelsey was a dupe.

Mary shook her head and smiled. She must have thought Kelsey was stupid too. "No, the real one. Kelsey didn't want to talk about it after she'd said she'd help me. All she wanted to know was how much money we had and when we were going away together."

I nodded and then shook my head. "Like a big dumb kid," I said. I hoped I never fell that way for someone who would use me.

Mary smiled. "Yeah. That was fine with me." She continued on merrily. When Mary got the checks, she deposited them to a dummy account with the same name as the fictitious company on the bogus purchase order. Then she got the money out again with a cash station card over a number of days. She redeposited the cash in a lot of little accounts at different banks to get around the reporting requirements for large deposits. Finally, Mary wrote checks from the little accounts to sweep the money she'd stolen into a master account in her own name. Mary had told Kelsey that she would move the money around in order to shield Kelsey from suspicion, but mostly it made cutting Kelsey out a lot easier and that was the final objective.

Mary sat back in her chair and smoked. She was talking to me like an old friend. She had told me the Secret and I had understood the necessity for radical action. "The problem with this scam was that Nealy needed a little money here and there, but I needed a lot and I knew we were going to get caught. I just planned to be gone before it happened. That was what Kelsey was for. When people started asking her questions, that was the fire alarm. I knew Kelsey was dumb enough to protect me until I could take off. But then she got killed and I had to hide out before I was ready." Mary laughed. "So here I am."

"Here you are," I agreed. "But I thought you were pretty attached to Kelsey. At least your letters were friendly enough."

"You've got to give a little to get a little. That's what she wanted to hear; so I gave it to her," said Mary.

What had Kelsey wanted to hear? Probably just that somebody loved her. I wondered why she hadn't wanted to hear it from Bev. When I looked at Mary, I saw a younger Bev, long-limbed, long-haired, exotic. I supposed Kelsey thought she could afford a newer model. I supposed that Mary was right about the way of the world, but it took her relationship with Kelsey to a whole other plane and it chipped away at my notion of Mary Tally as a kid who'd just been trying to even out the socio-economic score. I'd liked her when she told me that Kelsey couldn't buy her with a house and a white picket fence, but what she meant was just that the price wasn't high enough. I didn't like that.

"People who will sell their affections might do a lot of other things," I proposed. "Maybe you killed her."

Mary looked at me blankly, probably wondering why I was suddenly moralizing. "Why would I want to kill her?" she asked.

I went on with my accusations Hollywood detective-style, talking fast and tough, making up my theories as I talked. As I listened to myself, they sounded pretty good. "That's simple," I said. "Dead, Kelsey couldn't implicate you at all. No one would believe Nealy's claim that he was innocent; he'd had his hand in the cookie jar for years. Besides, he didn't know it was you embezzling. Kelsey knew though. You've already said you didn't love her so you flew to Chicago on Wednesday after work and you asked her to meet you at Gloria's. Or maybe she suggested Gloria's. It doesn't matter. You got there with your scarf and your dark glasses. You waited until it was time to leave and you shot her as you cut through the alley to the side street where she parked her car. Kelsey wasn't afraid of you and you could get really close to her so you didn't need a powerful gun. You could use a small one that would fit in the pocket of that jacket you're wearing now or in a purse. You're a smart girl, Mary," I said, "so you thought you'd make it look like a robbery and you took her fancy watch and the cash from her wallet, but you forgot her ring because you were in a hurry. Later that young punk from the neighborhood came across her body and took the ring figuring he could sell it to get high."

"That's the craziest thing I ever heard." Mary drained her espresso. She tossed her head with a thin kind of pride and I decided she was wearing a hair weave.

I took a leisurely drink of my beer. It was warm and getting flat. "Maybe so," I said, "but you got into work late, after ten Thursday morning and a six o'clock plane leaves Chicago and gets into Logan at nine-ten am every weekday morning, so you tell me how crazy it really is?"

Mary didn't venture an opinion on my theory. "Who the fuck are you really?" she said. "You can't be as stupid as you look. If I had killed her what would I be talking to you for? Lookit, Kelsey Beckett was a forty-two-year-old dyke with a thing for black women and access to a lot of cash. She backed me into a corner at a company party and I started getting ideas that I didn't have to work in that shitty accounting dungeon if I was smart. She had a use and we had some laughs, but my real lover and me, we had plans to be out of the country with the money before Kelsey knew what happened. This murder has really fucked up my plans every which way because I'm afraid to move my money now with the police sniffing around."

" 'This murder has really fucked up my plans?' " I repeated. "You're a nice girl, Mary. A woman you used to sleep with is shot and you're worried because it's an inconvenience?"

Mary Tally narrowed her eyes. She was not so pretty anymore, looking at me like I had slapped her.

"See this?" she said. She held both arms out in

front of her across the table. "It don't rub off. Remember, honey, you're still black whatever you got and so am I. You think I'm any colder than anybody's been to me?"

I didn't have an answer to that — not one that would have supported my righteousness, anyway. If life gave Mary Tally lemons, she made lemonade. She couldn't afford to get bogged down in morality and I had a good idea of how cold the world had been to her.

"Uhhuh." She worked her neck back and forth on her shoulders. "That's what I thought," she said. "What do you know about somebody wants to buy you for her entertainment? You think about that, girlfriend, before you start with me."

"All right," I said. "If you didn't, who do you think killed her?"

Mary Tally shrugged and tossed her store-bought hair again, satisfied I had been dressed down. "I just know it wasn't me. I've never even been to Chicago."

"What about the black woman at the bar the night she was killed?"

She shook her head. "Like I said, Kelsey liked black women. It could have been anybody."

Things were getting more confusing by the minute. I wasn't sure if I believed that Mary Tally hadn't ever been to Chicago, and hadn't killed Kelsey. But if she had, she was sure cool.

"I've got to go," Mary said before I could ask her anything else. "Thanks for lunch." She put her little bag over her shoulder and got up.

"Wait," I said. "We'll walk out together, all right?" I still had more questions.

She said "Okay," and when I opened my purse to pay the check she bolted around the table and down the stairs towards the exit.

I tried to follow but the waitress caught me by the elbow and handed me a bill. She was big enough to have rowed crew or played women's lacrosse. "Why don't you take care of this before you go," she said. She was smiling but it was more than a suggestion. I paid the bill and the burly waitress kept hold of my arm until I put her tip on the table.

Mary was gone. I walked out into Quincy Market hunting for her, but by then Mary Tally could have put herself so deep into the crowd that I could have looked all through next year and not found her. There was no point chasing a moving target. The only good thing was that compared to Susan, Mary Tally was a cheap date.

I hailed a cab back to Mary Tally's apartment house. That promised to be a waste of time, but it was worth a try. This time the Nose Ring looked at me through a peephole and talked to me through the closed front door. I knew it was Nose Ring. I recognized her voice.

"Mary Tally stood me up," I said. "I still have something for her."

"Well, leave it by the door and I'll see she gets it," Nose Ring said amiably.

"How do I know you'll give it to her," I complained. "You didn't give her the message before."

Nose Ring was an immovable object. "If Mary wants to talk to you, she's got your number." I think they both had my number by now.

"Great. I'll wait for her call." Nose Ring didn't answer so I figured the audience was over.

I headed back to the hotel. My room overlooked an atrium bar where I went for a drink since I'd run out of ideas about how to find Kelsey's killer. An older man by himself at the end of the bar was looking like he might come over so I paid my tab and left. I tried to call Bev, but she was still out so I ordered room service. There was a Cary Grant movie on television, the one where he's an artist who falls in love with a judge and I fell asleep to the clever dialogue.

XV

My phone rang at 1:30 am. The voice on the other end said, "Is Mary Tally dead, you fucker?" It was quite a wake-up call.

"Is this the girl with the nose ring?" I asked. "What are you talking about?"

"Just tell me, bitch. Is she dead?" It was Nose Ring and she was pissed.

"I don't know. I didn't kill her," I said, but she'd hung up by then.

That morning I checked out early, headed over to

Mary Tally's apartment and banged on the door until someone opened it. It was Nose Ring.

"I know it was you on the phone last night," I said.

She had been crying and she looked like she hadn't slept. Nose Ring stepped out into the hall. She was six feet tall if she was six inches and the veins on her arms stood up like mountain ranges on one of those textured maps.

"What the fuck do you want?" she said, and her tone was not friendly.

"I know it was you that called me last night," I said again.

Nose Ring looked at me. I had to raise my head to meet her stare. "What about it?" Her tone was menacing.

I told her I didn't appreciate the call due to the lateness of the hour and the salty language. It was the wrong thing to say. Nose Ring didn't look like she'd be fast but she was. Before I could take a step, she had my head tucked under the crook of her arm.

"Mary is dead," she hissed. "If you didn't kill her, then you got her killed and now I think you have five seconds to tell me one good reason why I shouldn't just twist your sorry head off of your shoulders."

"I'll scream loud," I offered, but apparently that was not compelling enough and Nose Ring began to twist my head until I felt my neck seize up. I screamed, but nobody on the hall even came to the door which shouldn't have surprised me, given the neighborhood.

"Look," I said. "I didn't kill Mary, but I came over here to find out who did." It wasn't exactly true, but it got the pain turned off. She let me go.

Actually, Nose Ring looked pretty deflated despite her assault. Whatever had happened to Mary Tally seemed to have taken all the spirit out of her, even if it hadn't removed the fight. I rolled my head and shoulders around to get reacquainted with them.

I was still standing at the front door. Nose Ring didn't even try to block my way and I took it as an invitation to make myself at home. Nose Ring followed me into her front room and threw herself into a big ratty chair.

"The place is a mess," Nose Ring apologized.

The decor was a cross between vintage radical lesbian chic and the Salvation Army. I took a seat on an old couch by the window. I liked the apartment. It was sunny and comfortable if a little rundown.

I said to Nose Ring, "Look. Are you all right?" I stopped short of touching her. My neck still hurt a lot.

She handed me a section of the *Globe* and looked like she might cry at any moment. The article was buried way in the back section and she must have gone over the paper in minute detail to find it. The headline read, Woman Sought in Embezzlement Case Found Dead near Faneuil Hall. It made me kind of sad that Kelsey rated a picture in the *Tribune* and feisty little Mary Tally's death was back page filler news. I would have felt worse about it, but I was starting to get scared.

"What's going on?" I asked.

Nose Ring ran her hand back and forth over the stubble on her head. "You know we were going to go away together at the end of the month. She just had to make sure that the accounts had cooled off and we were going to Mexico."

It wasn't the answer to my question, but things were starting to get clearer. "You wouldn't happen to be a video artist," I said.

She was.

"Okay," I said. "What's going on?"

"I thought you knew." Nose Ring blew her nose. I wondered if it hurt.

"So you called me this morning and accused me of killing Mary." I was getting the picture.

"No." Then she thought about it. "Well, yes and no," she said. "Somebody called me last night and said Mary was dead. It was before the paper came out. They said 'Mary Tally's dead.' I didn't know what to think, so I called you. Then today, this was in the paper."

"I met her at Quincy Market," I admitted. "We had lunch, sort of. But she ran out on me at the restaurant while I was trying to pay the bill. I didn't see her after that."

"I know," said Nose Ring. "She called me from a pay phone after you talked and said you were harmless and stupid."

"Thanks," I said.

"I was supposed to meet her later at a bar, Indigo in Cambridge, but she never came. When I got home, there was that message on the machine."

"I didn't call you and I didn't kill her," I said. "I was trying to find out who killed Kelsey myself."

"Then find out who killed Mary while you're at it, okay? Whoever killed her must have tracked her through you."

"I'll try," I said. I felt a little responsible for what happened to Mary. "But you have to tell me everything you know about Mary and Kelsey or I can't do much."

Nose Ring recited the same story that Mary had told me. She said she didn't know anything else and swore Mary had spent the night Kelsey was killed and most of the next morning rolling around in the sheets with her.

I didn't know how much of that I believed, but I was starting to get a pretty good idea of who had killed Mary. I didn't tell Nose Ring that. "Do me a favor," I said. "Don't mention to the police that I was here."

I dug in my purse and gave her two bills with pictures of Ulysses S. Grant on the fronts.

She took the money. "I told you," said Nose Ring. "I don't talk to the police. I already gave them a signed statement that I didn't know where Mary was. Besides, what am I going to tell them? I don't even know who you are."

She closed the door and my hundred dollars disappeared like magic. In a matter of days, I expected Nose Ring would vanish too and I wouldn't even be able to find her to tell her who I thought killed Mary.

XVI

It was noon and I had the cab take me straight to the airport even though I had a five-hour wait for my plane. The nice woman at the ticket counter put me on an earlier flight and I was starting to feel lucky. I hadn't had anything to eat since lunch with Mary and the mystery food on the flight tasted pretty good. I sat next to a massage therapist who was headed to China on an exchange program. I listened to her tell me her life story and wished that I were going to China. I was starting to get a lot of ideas that I didn't like.

When I got back to my apartment Sweet Potato's bowl was empty and the bottom was licked clean which was strange since he hates the dry food he gets when I'm away. He was happier than usual to see me and rubbed himself back and forth on my pants leg until the hair was so thick I had to brush it off in layers. I didn't mind; I was happy to see him too.

After I fed Sweet Potato and took a shower, I listened to the messages from Susan on my machine, promising that I would regret not coming back to her and inviting me to dinner in the same breath. I erased them. It seemed to me after lunch at Ramone's, I couldn't afford to let Susan take me out anymore.

I had a feeling in my gut that Bev had followed me to Boston and killed Mary Tally. Maybe because she hadn't been by to feed Sweet Potato. Maybe because she hadn't ever been home when I called to check in. Maybe because there just didn't seem to be anyone else left to have done it.

Maybe there was a mystery partner, but I didn't think so. Frankly, I didn't want to be convinced about Bev and I was looking for a way to disprove my own theories, because I just didn't know what I was going to do if it was true.

I poured myself a beer and then drove to Bev's apartment and put the top of my car up; the sky looked like rain. She wasn't home so I let myself in through the windowpane in her back door with the aid of a baseball bat I keep in my trunk.

In Bev's bedroom, the message light on her machine was blinking. I moved the stuffed animals, sat down on her bed and pressed the button to play the messages back. There were a lot, including three from me and a couple from her mother asking where she was. This was not the kind of evidence I wanted to see.

I really couldn't deny it was looking like Bev had killed Mary Tally, which was why she hadn't listened to her messages for two days and why Sweet Potato was so hungry. She had my flight numbers, and must have planned to get back to Chicago before me to feed Sweet Potato and make her house look lived in. I went straight to the bottom drawer in the kitchen for the gun, to be sure. It was there under the dish towel where I had seen her put it and it didn't look like it had been moved. I picked it up and put it on the kitchen counter. The ammunition was still on the top shelf of her linen closet under an electric blanket. I put that on the counter by the gun. Then I rooted around Bev's cabinets until I found her alcohol and I poured myself a gin and tonic, as the situation seemed to warrant something stiffer than beer.

I had problems, and I sat myself down on Bev's couch with the gun and the ammunition to think about how I was going to solve them. Sometimes alcohol is inspirational. This wasn't one of those times. I wasn't sure how I was going to explain the fact that I had let myself into Bev's apartment with a baseball bat, because if the gun was here, I had no idea how she'd killed Mary Tally. I wondered if I hadn't been wrong, but I still couldn't explain the phone messages or Sweet Potato's ravenous hunger. Bev's newspapers were still piled outside against the door.

I unloaded and loaded the gun a couple times,

until I got bored. Then I decided things would be better after I finished my drink. They weren't, so I just waited there on the couch in the dark. I must not have been made to be a private detective because I fell asleep waiting and was more surprised when Bev turned on the lights and found me than she was. It was a ridiculous picture: me curled up on the couch with the Louisville slugger I'd used as a pass-key and Bev standing in the open door. She carried an overnight bag with airline baggage stickers wrapped around the handle. I would have bet a month's pay that some of them said "Logan." I don't know what Sam Spade would have said, but I said, "Have a good trip?"

"What are you doing here, Ginny?"

I put my hand over my mouth and yawned. "Hanging out. Waiting for you to get in. Where have you been?"

"Nowhere," she said. "To the beach."

"The beach?" I raised my eyebrows. "I think we have to talk, Bev."

She sat down across from me on her loveseat and put a coaster under the glass I'd left on the coffee table. I thought I really needed the drink to get through this, but it was probably all water by now.

"About what?" Bev asked.

I had to hand it to her. She looked genuinely baffled. I was beginning to think maybe I was crazy, but no other scenario fit and as much as I didn't want to believe it, my guts were telling me she had killed Mary Tally. I just didn't know why.

"You've been in Boston. I know because you were the only one who knew I was going and you didn't feed Sweet Potato. He was starved when I got home and there are a million messages from all weekend on your machine. I think you followed me and killed that girl." Listening to myself, I thought my logic sounded a little ridiculous. My voice was high and hysterical. I felt not at all like Hercule Poirot and hoped that Bev would give me a reasonable explanation for everything to take me off the hook.

She didn't, of course.

Bev shrugged. "I had to kill her. She made me kill Kelsey." Her voice was calm and conversational, just like the crazed killers in the movies. "She seduced Kelsey into stealing to keep her when she could have been happy with me. That Mary Tally killed her by making her stop wanting me as surely as if she'd shot Kelsey herself. How happy could she have been with that girl? I put Kelsey out of her misery."

That was some logic. I shook my head. "Wait, Bev. You killed Kelsey?" This was more than I had bargained for and I was having trouble coping.

"I'm glad you understand," Bev smiled. She reached across the coffee table and gave my hand a squeeze.

"What happened?" I was flabbergasted.

"It was an accident. I found the letter and I asked her about it. Kelsey said that she and Mary were in love and they would be living together. I asked her what Mary had that I didn't and she couldn't tell me."

I thought about Mary Tally; I could have told her, but it didn't seem appropriate.

Bev started to cry. "Kelsey said we would be friends and I would get over it. Oh, but Ginny," she said, "Kelsey was exactly what I wanted. We were perfect for each other. I could never get over her in a million years. You know this has been such a strain on me. I'm not sure I'll meet my yearly sales goals and then I can kiss goodbye to my bonus."

I nodded. Things were tough all over.

Bev brought a box of Kleenex from the kitchen and dried her eyes. "You can't imagine what it was like. When I told Kelsey I couldn't let her go, she just walked out. I followed her to Gloria's place."

"And you were wearing a headwrap," I said.

"I didn't have time to do my hair," Bev explained, "and of course my eyes were a mess; I'd been crying so much." It was absurd that Bev was disguised because she didn't have her look together, sort of a "twist of fate, stranger than fiction" kind of thing. It was so like Bev that I believed her.

"What happened at the bar?" As Bev talked to me, I felt like one of those little animals you see on the road at night, who can't move out of the way of your car because they are hypnotized by the headlights. It was a story I couldn't turn away from, much as I would have liked to.

"She didn't want to go with me at first, but I told her I'd make a scene and the police would come. Kelsey was afraid of a scene so she went with me to the alley behind the bar, she said I could say what I had to say there. I begged her to come home with me, but she wouldn't. She said maybe I should move out. I took the gun out of my purse to scare her. Then she said, definitely I should move out because she didn't love me any more. Then the gun went off. I don't know how. Kelsey looked down and saw she was shot in the stomach. She screamed but the music from the bar was so loud, I don't think anyone heard. It sounded like an animal. She didn't seem that hurt, just mad. I'd never seen anyone so angry and she frightened me. She was coming at me saying she'd kill me so I just started firing the gun. The shots came fast, one after another in her stomach. I don't remember how many there were, but after a while Kelsey fell over. She wasn't dead, but she was hurt and cursing. There was a lot of blood." Bev hugged herself at the shoulders. "It made me sick. Then Kelsey said I was going to jail forever when the police found out what I'd done. I left her there because I had to get away from her to think."

"I can see how you might feel that way," I said, making a real effort to see things from Bev's perspective.

Bev nodded in agreement. "You see, don't you, how I didn't know what to do then. So I walked back to my car and sat there for a while. When I checked my hair in the rearview mirror, I realized that with the scarf and the dark glasses no one would recognize me. I hid them in the trunk of my car. Then I went back around to the alley. Kelsey was still there but she was weaker and her voice was barely above a whisper. She demanded I call her an ambulance that minute. I almost did. But she was so nasty. She told me again I was going to jail. Ginny, I just couldn't go to jail, so I closed my eyes and shot her until there were no more bullets in the gun. I took her watch and her keys. I took her cash and threw her wallet in the dumpster. Then I called you from the pay phone in front of Gloria's because I needed to talk to someone and I didn't know what to do. I was going to tell you what happened to Kelsey but then I didn't. You were so drunk so I just went home. The police came at five that morning and I thought they must have found out I shot her. But they just wanted into her apartment. They had no idea we were lovers. I told them the last time I saw Kelsey was after dinner. They didn't search. They seemed satisfied and went away. Then you called and asked if there was anything you could do. I couldn't bear to see the gun so I asked you to take it."

"Let me get this straight," I said. "You tried to give me the gun you shot Kelsey with?"

"It was an accident. I didn't mean to shoot her and then she was so hateful I didn't know what to do. She tried to kill me," Bev said with emphasis. "But I knew the police didn't know me and wouldn't understand."

"You asked me to keep the gun you shot Kelsey with?" I picked up the thing from the counter and dropped it on her coffee table. "This gun?" I didn't want to believe that Bev had tried to set me up, but it was very hard not to. The thought was making me very irritable. I felt like I had PMS and wasn't due for two weeks.

"I didn't want to throw it away yet," she explained reasonably. "I was trying to decide whether to turn myself in. But I couldn't do that until Mary Tally was gone. You understand."

"So you tried to give it to me?" I didn't understand.

"I knew I could trust you to keep it for me and not tell anybody," Bev said. The thing I hated was she had been right. "Mary ruined Kelsey's life — who else was there to punish her?"

"The police," I offered.

Bev shook her head. "How could they punish her enough?" she asked, but it seemed to me being dead on some side street near Faneuil Hall might be a bit excessive.

Then I was confused. "How did you kill Mary Tally if your gun was here all weekend?" It crossed my mind that Bev could be delusional. It was a comforting thought and I pursued it. "Are you sure you really killed Kelsey and Mary?"

"Oh, I just bought another gun," said Bev. "A bigger one. That little one wasn't very effective on Kelsey and I didn't think Mary Tally would hold still for long for me to shoot her enough times to kill her."

Her logic was startling, which only goes to show you, being crazy doesn't make you stupid.

"Where's the gun now?" I asked.

Bev looked at me as if I were the crazy one. "I threw it in the Charles River last night. I didn't need it anymore."

"Right," I said. "Tell me again how you found Mary."

"Like you said, I followed you to Boston, to her house, to Quincy Market." Bev spoke slowly, as if she were explaining to a particularly stupid child or someone who didn't speak the language. "When she left you, I followed her. She laughed at me when I asked if she was in love with Kelsey, so I shot her. I was going to anyway, but I could feel like she deserved it more because of her snotty attitude. I'm not sorry; she killed Kelsey," Bev insisted.

"No, you killed Kelsey, Bev," I said. There no point in going on. She was clearly crazy; you have to be crazy to kill somebody, it seems to me, and I was sick to death of craziness. "Nobody else, just you." I pointed to the gun. "See, look at this," I said. "Come on, let's just call the police and take care of this. I promise we will get you some help."

"Ginny, I can't go to jail," said Bev. It made her cry just to think about it and pretty soon she was sobbing. The tears ran after each other in trails down her face and her makeup washed away.

I almost felt sorry for her, but she'd made her bed. People think tears are a sign of weakness, but they're wrong. Sometimes they're an expression of desperation. Animals who can't see their way out of a box cry and it is a pitiable noise. This was the sound Bev was making.

I forced my voice to be as friendly and supportive as possible, given that I wasn't feeling at all friendly or supportive, given that I was turning her in.

"Of course you're not going to jail," I said. "We're going to get you some help."

I was of the sincere understanding that we do not send crazy people to jail. I imagined that Bev would be placed in some comfortable prison for people who are basically harmless unless they are riled.

"We're going to make sure you get some help, okay?" I said, and I put out my hand for her to take hold of.

"Bull Shit," said Bev. Bev didn't usually curse, so I knew she was adamant. "I'm not going to jail."

I didn't think our talk was going well.

In the movies, the murderer has to give up once you've caught him. It's a rule. The murderer sits resigned while the hero calls the police. This wasn't the movies and I wasn't fast enough to stop her. Bev reached out and picked up the gun from the coffee table. She pointed it at me with more conviction than I was comfortable with.

"Stand up," she said.

I kept my seat and tried to stare her down. I couldn't remember if I had unloaded the gun when I was playing with it.

"You know, that's not even loaded," I lied.

Bev shut her eyes for a moment and fired into one of her wood parquet floor tiles. In the movies the hero would rush the murderer at this point when his guard was down, wrestling the gun from his hands in a long harrowing struggle. This wasn't the movies. All I could do was look at the smoking hole in the floor and hope I didn't soil myself.

"Okay," I said, "I lied, but let's not get excited. You were going to turn yourself in; I was just trying to help you do what's right." I tried to smile as if we were having a friendly disagreement. We were friends after all, I reminded her.

Bev kept the gun pointed level with my chest.

"Let's just call the police," I suggested. "I'm sure they'll understand."

She shook her head. "I don't think I should be punished for an accident. I think I've suffered enough. You're my friend, you should understand that."

"Bev," I said. "Remember when you told me I was your best friend?" Apparently she didn't. "I'm still your best friend."

"Put your hands above your head, Ginny, and turn around." We'd clearly been watching the same old movies. Nick Charles, the Thin Man, would have put his hands over his head as he was told. So would Sam Spade and Philip Marlowe, Nancy Drew and every Pinkerton detective there ever was. So did I.

"Walk slowly to the front door and open it," Bev advised me. I could feel the nose of the little gun in the small of my back. Every so often Bev would stick me with it and then apologize, if I didn't move fast enough. I did what she said.

The street was empty when I opened the door. No cars, no people, no clouds, no saviors. The sky was clear and black. It looked like a planetarium star show. She walked me to the curb.

At this point, in the movies something usually happens. Ideally the police would show up with Myrna Loy at the front of the pack holding Asta and shouting "Nicky," for the villain, unable to live with his wicked deeds, would turn the gun on himself and conveniently expire. None of these things seemed likely. With Bev's gun poking my back, I began to realize that whatever happened here to save me, I was going to have to orchestrate it all by myself.

So, I ran. As hard as I could with my loafers slapping the pavement and my arms pumping down the middle of the street. For a moment, I thought I was going to get away. I was wrong. My legs came out from under me mid-stride and I grabbed with both hands at the one where I'd been shot, hitting the pavement with my cheek and sliding into the gutter. Bev had managed to shoot me in the back of the calf. The pain was so bad I almost didn't care that she was standing over me, taking aim at my head.

"I'm sorry." Bev's mouth was moving but her words were on a seven-second delay between my ears and my brain. "I'm really sorry," she said. "I didn't mean it, Ginny. But I just can't go to jail."

"I'm sorry too," I managed to say.

Bev let the gun hang limp at the end of her arm. "Ginny, if you could just forget this happened, I think we can work this out." She was whipped and crying, but with the gun in her hand I thought she had a compelling argument that I ought to at least think about. "All we have now is each other," she said.

It was exactly what I'd been wanting to hear for months, years, and I wondered if she meant it. As much as I loved Bev, her words sounded as crazy as the promises Susan kept leaving on my phone machine. The difference was, I wanted to hear these crazy lies from Bev. But I couldn't forget Mary Tally. I couldn't even forget about Kelsey and it put me in an ugly box.

"I can't believe this is happening." Bev held her arms out, open, with the gun hanging limp at the end of one of them.

"I'm sorry," I said again. I couldn't believe it either. I tried to think of a way out of this situation that didn't involve jail or death.

The moon had gone behind the clouds and I felt like I was donating blood to the sidewalk. From down the street Susan was running towards us, moving her lips and waving her arms over her head. I waited for the words to reach me.

"You shot her," Susan said. Her lips were busy

161

again and her eyes were wild, wilder than Bev's under the street light. "I saw you shoot her," she was shouting.

Bev looked down at the gun in her hand as if someone else had put it there. But she was stopped and boxed in, like me, by the craziness of her situation, hypnotized by the waving of Susan's arms.

"I saw you shoot her," Susan was screaming.

"It's all right." I tried to stand but my legs wouldn't hold me up. I fell again and my hands made a red print on the cement gutter like something on the sidewalk in front of Grauman's Chinese Theater. "It's going to be all right," I said. But I couldn't speak. My ears were ringing and I couldn't hear myself.

"I've called the police," Susan was saying, it seemed from very far away.

"I'm fine," I said. The ends of my fingers and toes felt like they belonged on someone else.

Bev dropped the gun. She turned and ran out into the street while the world receded slowly with a dull thud and a terminal squeal.

They say people who think they are about to die have that split-second of clarity filled with revelations about their lives. Mine was the hazy thought that I couldn't imagine which would be worse: being dead or hearing Naomi say "I told you so." I wondered how embarrassing it would be when my folks came to clean out my apartment and discovered my subscription to *On Our Backs* which I read for the thought-provoking articles on differently-pleasured women. I was hoping for some divine intervention when I thought I heard Susan calling my name.

Fortunately, my parents were spared the discourse on pierced genitalia. Unfortunately, when I woke up in the hospital, Naomi was on hand to put her two cents in. "What the hell," she said cheerfully. "There's a dance in the old girl yet."

I couldn't help but smile. "*Toujours gai.*" But I lacked conviction. I couldn't feel my leg and I wasn't brave enough to ask about it.

I surmised this was the hospital, that or heaven, but probably the hospital since they'd let Naomi in. Everything was white and quiet except for the face and the baritone voice of some fresh-faced resident who was looking down at me. He was handsome and tall, the kind of professional black man suitor my father had been praying for. If I were straight it would have been a great way to wake up.

"How are we feeling, young lady?" he said.

We were feeling none too well. "Jesus," I said. "What happened?"

"You've been through quite a lot —" The resident consulted my chart, "Virginia." He seemed proud that he could find my name among all the other bits of information. "The police would like to talk to you, if you feel well enough."

Naomi stood up behind him and shook her head from side to side.

I shook my head in the way she indicated. "I'm very tired," I said. "Can it wait a little while?"

She was shaking her head vigorously up and down now. Yes, this was clearly the correct response. Naomi was pleased.

But the doctor frowned. "They like to talk to victims as soon as possible, but at least they have the statements from your friends."

Naomi bobbed her head.

"I'm sorry," I said again. "But I'm very tired right now."

The doctor nodded as if this was understandable.

"I have some information from your family," said Naomi. I thought that was odd since Naomi had never met my family.

She turned to the doctor and said, "It's a little private."

The doctor smiled. "Five minutes," he said over his shoulder as he walked out with his white coat flapping. I thought he was too young to be so officious, but his attitude was no business of mine.

"What's with him?" I asked Naomi when he had left.

Naomi closed the door and giggled. "I told him I was your lover."

"Great. What's going on," I said.

"Bev tried to kill you," explained Naomi.

"I know that part," I said. "How did I get here?"

"Dumb luck," Naomi said. "If you hadn't noticed, Susan follows you everywhere. She was staking out your apartment when you got back from Boston. She followed you to Bev's and when she saw Bev come home and you didn't come out, she listened at the door. Then, she heard the business about the gun. So, she ran to a pay phone and called me and the cops in that order."

"How did you know I was in Boston?" I asked.

"You weren't home all weekend, Ginny. It didn't take a rocket scientist to figure out you'd try to play Nancy Drew. But look," Naomi said. "Tell me what exactly happened and I'll tell you what we're going to tell the police."

164

"Thanks a lot," I said. I was getting sick of Naomi's bunker mentality. "I thought I'd just tell them the truth."

"The truth?" Naomi rolled her eyes. "With the mail tampering and the trip to Boston. You know Mary Tally's dead?"

I said I knew. "I was thinking I'd omit the mail tampering and my personal investigation," I admitted.

"Well, that's what I'm saying," explained Naomi. "Tell me what happened and I'll tell you what we need to tell the police."

I told her the story of the gun and Bev's confession, complete with the trip to Boston and my breaking and entering. "What's going to happen to Bev?" I asked. "She wasn't really going to kill me."

"There's nothing you can do about that." Naomi closed her eyes and I thought for a minute she'd been crying. But when she opened them again she looked like her old pragmatic self. It took Naomi about a minute flat to dream up a sanitized version of history in which I was innocent of any chargeable offenses. She made me repeat the story for her over and over and she slapped me on the arm when I got it right. "Good girl," she said, as if she were training a dog.

"What's going to happen to Bev?" I said.

Naomi took a breath. "Bev's dead," she said. "That's the rest of it. So, you'd better take care of yourself. Susan spooked her while she was trying to kill you and she ran out into the street."

I couldn't speak.

"I got there as soon as I could," Naomi said. "It didn't take a brain surgeon to figure out what

165

happened and confidentially, I thought Bev did it all along. No hard feelings, Ginny." She closed her eyes and sighed. "But when Susan ran up on you, Bev just flipped out. And Susan was still screaming when I got there; you can imagine. She says Bev dropped the gun and ran out into the street toward her apartment. By this time you'd lost enough blood to be down for the count and a cab hits Bev right in front of her door. The guy didn't speak a bit of English, stone cold sober, just hit her coming around the corner and he's blubbering away in some foreign language, crying over the hood of his cab. The police are standing around like they think it's some kind of freak show and it took two guys to quiet Susan down because all the time she's screaming that you're both dead. They put you and Bev in an ambulance and you know the rest now."

Naomi recrossed her legs and looked around the room. "I'm sorry," she said as kind of an afterthought. "You'd think they'd have an ashtray around here for visitors."

"I don't think they want you to smoke in here." But I handed her my water glass. "Bev wasn't trying to kill me."

"That could be," Naomi said. "I've heard of stranger things." She smoked thoughtfully. Naomi is a woman of private emotions. She studied her hands while I cried. My mouth was dry and I was sorry to have given up my glass to Naomi for an ashtray.

"Don't you want to know what happened to your leg," she said finally.

I had forgotten about my leg. "All right." I was starting to feel genuinely tired. "What happened to my leg?"

"It's fine. There were splinters of bone but they got them out," Naomi said. "That doctor you met got them out. That's one good thing."

"That's good," I agreed.

Naomi smiled. It was a thin watery expression and she blinked hard to keep her eyes from tearing up.

XVII

Weeks later, Naomi was sucking the salt off the free pretzels at the Penguin, resting her feet on the brass rail at the bottom of the bar, looking past me at her reflection in the mirror. I propped myself up beside her against the bar and laid my crutches down on an empty stool. Some tough girls were playing pool across the room against a team of bankers wearing weekend leather in the Sunday Women's Sports League. They were playing for keeps and the bankers were winning, surprisingly. I watched them sink their last ball while the tough girls rocked on their heels praying for a miracle that didn't come.

Naomi smoothed down the top of her hair and smiled at herself with satisfaction. "Your beer is getting warm." She patted my hand maternally. "Don't drink it. I'll buy you another one."

Naomi had been buying all afternoon. The day before she had treated me to the movies. Before I could stop her, she waved for the bartender to keep the beer coming. I finished off the warm one anyway. Waste not, want not.

"Are you all right?" Naomi asked.

I was fine. My life had managed to reconstitute itself except for Naomi's recent bout of generosity and the hole Bev had left that Naomi couldn't seem to fill. I don't mean of course the hole in my leg which it turned out was almost fortuitous. Since the real story was a little long to go into, I'd given out for simplicity's sake that my bullet wound was the result of my resisting a mugging. It was a story that had grown in the retelling, and the hole in my leg had made me something of a hero at Whytebread. I had for the first time in my career the political popularity of say a twenty handicap golfer, and the Managing Director who previously could not remember my name confided in the hall that he had always known I had the kind of stuff Whytebread wanted to see from their young Turks. So much for the celebrated hole in my leg.

The hole in my heart is another thing, but my life is nothing but shady calm now that people want to take care of me. Ellen Borgia and even Starr rushed out to send flowers during my short convalescence. Susan sent more flowers and a long, winding note written in the white spaces of a get-well card, explaining why she couldn't see me anymore. Craziness. Naomi camped out in my apartment eating my food, with her feet up on the furniture and smoking endless packs of cigarettes, until I worried that the walls would turn gray from the smoke.

I was saying to Naomi, "Maybe craziness and order chase each other through our lives like seasons." She looked at me strangely through her smoke, half-listening as she is wont to do.

"You know," I said, "like boom and bust. 'A time to sow and a time to reap.'" But sadly that was all I could remember of *Ecclesiastes*. It is an old man's book, short because time is very short, and I was feeling very old, thinking craziness was kind of a segue so that you can better appreciate peace, a squall on the lake made up to blow over, leaving nothing but a clear eye through which to view the world. A good thing really.

Em has come back to me. Now we live apart and sleep together. No surprise in a universe where tongues heal faster than hearts. But Bev is gone and I keep missing her. It's funny how strangers on a familiar street can look just like old friends until you look more closely, or how things you'd thought you'd forgotten can come back so suddenly that your words surprise you. "'Generations come and generations go while the earth endures forever. The sun rises and the sun goes down; then it speeds to its place and rises there again.'" My reflection looked back across the bar at me, moving its lips, and I smiled in spite of myself as if I'd gotten a present I hadn't expected.

"Philosophy will give you an ulcer," Naomi said by way of friendly advice. She pinched my arm hard and ordered me another beer.

A few of the publications of
THE NAIAD PRESS, INC.
P.O. Box 10543 • Tallahassee, Florida 32302
Phone (904) 539-5965
Mail orders welcome. Please include 15% postage.

IN THE GAME by Nikki Baker. 192 pp. A Virginia Kelly
mystery. First in a series.   ISBN 01-56280-004-3 $8.95

AVALON by Mary Jane Jones. 240 pp. A Lesbian Arthurian
romance.   ISBN 0-941483-96-7   9.95

STRANDED by Camarin Grae. 384 pp. Entertaining, riveting
adventure.   ISBN 0-941483-99-1   9.95

THE DAUGHTERS OF ARTEMIS by Lauren Wright Douglas.
240 pp. Third Caitlin Reece mystery.   ISBN 0-941483-95-9   8.95

CLEARWATER by Catherine Ennis. 176 pp. Romantic secrets
of a small Louisiana town.   ISBN 0-941483-65-7   8.95

THE HALLELUJAH MURDERS by Dorothy Tell. 176 pp.
Second Poppy Dillworth mystery.   ISBN 0-941483-88-6   8.95

ZETA BASE by Judith Alguire. 208 pp. Lesbian triangle
on a future Earth.   ISBN 0-941483-94-0   9.95

SECOND CHANCE by Jackie Calhoun. 256 pp. Contemporary
Lesbian lives and loves.   ISBN 0-941483-93-2   9.95

MURDER BY TRADITION by Katherine V. Forrest. 288 pp.
A Kate Delafield Mystery. 4th in a series.   ISBN 0-941483-89-4   18.95

BENEDICTION by Diane Salvatore. 272 pp. Striking,
contemporary romantic novel.   ISBN 0-941483-90-8   9.95

CALLING RAIN by Karen Marie Christa Minns. 240 pp.
Spellbinding, erotic love story   ISBN 0-941483-87-8   9.95

BLACK IRIS by Jeane Harris. 192 pp. Caroline's hidden past . . .
                                                ISBN 0-941483-68-1   8.95

TOUCHWOOD by Karin Kallmaker. 240 pp. Loving, May/
December romance.   ISBN 0-941483-76-2   8.95

BAYOU CITY SECRETS by Deborah Powell. 224 pp. A Hollis
Carpenter mystery. First in a series.   ISBN 0-941483-91-6   8.95

COP OUT by Claire McNab. 208 pp. 4th Det. Insp. Carol Ashton
mystery.   ISBN 0-941483-84-3   8.95

LODESTAR by Phyllis Horn. 224 pp. Romantic, fast-moving
adventure.   ISBN 0-941483-83-5   8.95

THE BEVERLY MALIBU by Katherine V. Forrest. 288 pp. A
Kate Delafield Mystery. 3rd in a series. (HC)   ISBN 0-941483-47-9   16.95
                              Paperback   ISBN 0-941483-48-7   9.95

THAT OLD STUDEBAKER by Lee Lynch. 272 pp. Andy's affair
with Regina and her attachment to her beloved car.
ISBN 0-941483-82-7   9.95

PASSION'S LEGACY by Lori Paige. 224 pp. Sarah is swept into
the arms of Augusta Pym in this delightful historical romance.
ISBN 0-941483-81-9   8.95

THE PROVIDENCE FILE by Amanda Kyle Williams. 256 pp.
Second espionage thriller featuring lesbian agent Madison McGuire
ISBN 0-941483-92-4   8.95

I LEFT MY HEART by Jaye Maiman. 320 pp. A Robin Miller
Mystery. First in a series.   ISBN 0-941483-72-X   9.95

THE PRICE OF SALT by Patricia Highsmith (writing as Claire
Morgan). 288 pp. Classic lesbian novel, first issued in 1952 . . .
acknowledged by its author under her own, very famous, name.
ISBN 1-56280-003-5   8.95

SIDE BY SIDE by Isabel Miller. 256 pp. From beloved author of
Patience and Sarah.   ISBN 0-941483-77-0   8.95

SOUTHBOUND by Sheila Ortiz Taylor. 240 pp. Hilarious sequel
to *Faultline.*   ISBN 0-941483-78-9   8.95

STAYING POWER: LONG TERM LESBIAN COUPLES
by Susan E. Johnson. 352 pp. Joys of coupledom.
ISBN 0-941-483-75-4   12.95

SLICK by Camarin Grae. 304 pp. Exotic, erotic adventure.
ISBN 0-941483-74-6   9.95

NINTH LIFE by Lauren Wright Douglas. 256 pp. A Caitlin
Reece mystery. 2nd in a series.   ISBN 0-941483-50-9   8.95

PLAYERS by Robbi Sommers. 192 pp. Sizzling, erotic novel.
ISBN 0-941483-73-8   8.95

MURDER AT RED ROOK RANCH by Dorothy Tell. 224 pp.
First Poppy Dillworth adventure.   ISBN 0-941483-80-0   8.95

LESBIAN SURVIVAL MANUAL by Rhonda Dicksion.
112 pp. Cartoons!   ISBN 0-941483-71-1   8.95

A ROOM FULL OF WOMEN by Elisabeth Nonas. 256 pp.
Contemporary Lesbian lives.   ISBN 0-941483-69-X   8.95

MURDER IS RELATIVE by Karen Saum. 256 pp. The first
Brigid Donovan mystery.   ISBN 0-941483-70-3   8.95

PRIORITIES by Lynda Lyons 288 pp. Science fiction with
a twist.   ISBN 0-941483-66-5   8.95

THEME FOR DIVERSE INSTRUMENTS by Jane Rule. 208
pp. Powerful romantic lesbian stories.   ISBN 0-941483-63-0   8.95

LESBIAN QUERIES by Hertz & Ertman. 112 pp. The questions
you were too embarrassed to ask.   ISBN 0-941483-67-3   8.95

CLUB 12 by Amanda Kyle Williams. 288 pp. Espionage thriller
featuring a lesbian agent!   ISBN 0-941483-64-9   8.95

DEATH DOWN UNDER by Claire McNab. 240 pp. 3rd Det.
Insp. Carol Ashton mystery.   ISBN 0-941483-39-8   8.95

MONTANA FEATHERS by Penny Hayes. 256 pp. Vivian and
Elizabeth find love in frontier Montana.   ISBN 0-941483-61-4   8.95

CHESAPEAKE PROJECT by Phyllis Horn. 304 pp. Jessie &
Meredith in perilous adventure.   ISBN 0-941483-58-4   8.95

LIFESTYLES by Jackie Calhoun. 224 pp. Contemporary Lesbian
lives and loves.   ISBN 0-941483-57-6   8.95

VIRAGO by Karen Marie Christa Minns. 208 pp. Darsen has
chosen Ginny.   ISBN 0-941483-56-8   8.95

WILDERNESS TREK by Dorothy Tell. 192 pp. Six women on
vacation learning "new" skills.   ISBN 0-941483-60-6   8.95

MURDER BY THE BOOK by Pat Welch. 256 pp. A Helen
Black Mystery. First in a series.   ISBN 0-941483-59-2   8.95

BERRIGAN by Vicki P. McConnell. 176 pp. Youthful Lesbian —
romantic, idealistic Berrigan.   ISBN 0-941483-55-X   8.95

LESBIANS IN GERMANY by Lillian Faderman & B. Eriksson.
128 pp. Fiction, poetry, essays.   ISBN 0-941483-62-2   8.95

THERE'S SOMETHING I'VE BEEN MEANING TO TELL
YOU Ed. by Loralee MacPike. 288 pp. Gay men and lesbians
coming out to their children.   ISBN 0-941483-44-4   9.95
                                             ISBN 0-941483-54-1   16.95

LIFTING BELLY by Gertrude Stein. Ed. by Rebecca Mark. 104
pp. Erotic poetry.   ISBN 0-941483-51-7   8.95
                                             ISBN 0-941483-53-3   14.95

ROSE PENSKI by Roz Perry. 192 pp. Adult lovers in a long-term
relationship.   ISBN 0-941483-37-1   8.95

AFTER THE FIRE by Jane Rule. 256 pp. Warm, human novel
by this incomparable author.   ISBN 0-941483-45-2   8.95

SUE SLATE, PRIVATE EYE by Lee Lynch. 176 pp. The gay
folk of Peacock Alley are *all cats*.   ISBN 0-941483-52-5   8.95

CHRIS by Randy Salem. 224 pp. Golden oldie. Handsome Chris
and her adventures.   ISBN 0-941483-42-8   8.95

THREE WOMEN by March Hastings. 232 pp. Golden oldie. A
triangle among wealthy sophisticates.   ISBN 0-941483-43-6   8.95

RICE AND BEANS by Valeria Taylor. 232 pp. Love and
romance on poverty row.   ISBN 0-941483-41-X   8.95

PLEASURES by Robbi Sommers. 204 pp. Unprecedented
eroticism.   ISBN 0-941483-49-5   8.95

EDGEWISE by Camarin Grae. 372 pp. Spellbinding
adventure.   ISBN 0-941483-19-3   9.95

FATAL REUNION by Claire McNab. 224 pp. 2nd Det. Inspec.
Carol Ashton mystery.   ISBN 0-941483-40-1   8.95

KEEP TO ME STRANGER by Sarah Aldridge. 372 pp. Romance
set in a department store dynasty.   ISBN 0-941483-38-X   9.95

HEARTSCAPE by Sue Gambill. 204 pp. American lesbian in
Portugal.   ISBN 0-941483-33-9   8.95

IN THE BLOOD by Lauren Wright Douglas. 252 pp. Lesbian
science fiction adventure fantasy   ISBN 0-941483-22-3   8.95

THE BEE'S KISS by Shirley Verel. 216 pp. Delicate, delicious
romance.   ISBN 0-941483-36-3   8.95

RAGING MOTHER MOUNTAIN by Pat Emmerson. 264 pp.
Furosa Firechild's adventures in Wonderland. ISBN 0-941483-35-5   8.95

IN EVERY PORT by Karin Kallmaker. 228 pp. Jessica's sexy,
adventuresome travels.   ISBN 0-941483-37-7   8.95

OF LOVE AND GLORY by Evelyn Kennedy. 192 pp. Exciting
WWII romance.   ISBN 0-941483-32-0   8.95

CLICKING STONES by Nancy Tyler Glenn. 288 pp. Love
transcending time.   ISBN 0-941483-31-2   9.95

SURVIVING SISTERS by Gail Pass. 252 pp. Powerful love
story.   ISBN 0-941483-16-9   8.95

SOUTH OF THE LINE by Catherine Ennis. 216 pp. Civil War
adventure.   ISBN 0-941483-29-0   8.95

WOMAN PLUS WOMAN by Dolores Klaich. 300 pp. Supurb
Lesbian overview.   ISBN 0-941483-28-2   9.95

SLOW DANCING AT MISS POLLY'S by Sheila Ortiz Taylor.
96 pp. Lesbian Poetry   ISBN 0-941483-30-4   7.95

DOUBLE DAUGHTER by Vicki P. McConnell. 216 pp. A Nyla
Wade Mystery, third in the series.   ISBN 0-941483-26-6   8.95

HEAVY GILT by Delores Klaich. 192 pp. Lesbian detective/
disappearing homophobes/upper class gay society.

                                              ISBN 0-941483-25-8   8.95

THE FINER GRAIN by Denise Ohio. 216 pp. Brilliant young
college lesbian novel.   ISBN 0-941483-11-8   8.95

THE AMAZON TRAIL by Lee Lynch. 216 pp. Life, travel & lore
of famous lesbian author.   ISBN 0-941483-27-4   8.95

HIGH CONTRAST by Jessie Lattimore. 264 pp. Women of the
Crystal Palace.   ISBN 0-941483-17-7   8.95

OCTOBER OBSESSION by Meredith More. Josie's rich, secret
Lesbian life.   ISBN 0-941483-18-5   8.95

LESBIAN CROSSROADS by Ruth Baetz. 276 pp. Contemporary
Lesbian lives.   ISBN 0-941483-21-5   9.95

BEFORE STONEWALL: THE MAKING OF A GAY AND
LESBIAN COMMUNITY by Andrea Weiss & Greta Schiller.
96 pp., 25 illus.   ISBN 0-941483-20-7   7.95

WE WALK THE BACK OF THE TIGER by Patricia A. Murphy.
192 pp. Romantic Lesbian novel/beginning women's movement.
                                           ISBN 0-941483-13-4   8.95

SUNDAY'S CHILD by Joyce Bright. 216 pp. Lesbian athletics, at
last the novel about sports.   ISBN 0-941483-12-6   8.95

OSTEN'S BAY by Zenobia N. Vole. 204 pp. Sizzling adventure
romance set on Bonaire.   ISBN 0-941483-15-0   8.95

LESSONS IN MURDER by Claire McNab. 216 pp. 1st Det. Inspec.
Carol Ashton mystery — erotic tension!.   ISBN 0-941483-14-2   8.95

YELLOWTHROAT by Penny Hayes. 240 pp. Margarita, bandit,
kidnaps Julia.   ISBN 0-941483-10-X   8.95

SAPPHISTRY: THE BOOK OF LESBIAN SEXUALITY by
Pat Califia. 3d edition, revised. 208 pp. ISBN 0-941483-24-X   8.95

CHERISHED LOVE by Evelyn Kennedy. 192 pp. Erotic
Lesbian love story.   ISBN 0-941483-08-8   8.95

LAST SEPTEMBER by Helen R. Hull. 208 pp. Six stories & a
glorious novella.   ISBN 0-941483-09-6   8.95

THE SECRET IN THE BIRD by Camarin Grae. 312 pp. Striking,
psychological suspense novel.   ISBN 0-941483-05-3   8.95

TO THE LIGHTNING by Catherine Ennis. 208 pp. Romantic
Lesbian 'Robinson Crusoe' adventure.   ISBN 0-941483-06-1   8.95

THE OTHER SIDE OF VENUS by Shirley Verel. 224 pp.
Luminous, romantic love story.   ISBN 0-941483-07-X   8.95

DREAMS AND SWORDS by Katherine V. Forrest. 192 pp.
Romantic, erotic, imaginative stories.   ISBN 0-941483-03-7   8.95

MEMORY BOARD by Jane Rule. 336 pp. Memorable novel
about an aging Lesbian couple.   ISBN 0-941483-02-9   9.95

THE ALWAYS ANONYMOUS BEAST by Lauren Wright
Douglas. 224 pp. A Caitlin Reece mystery. First in a series.
                                           ISBN 0-941483-04-5   8.95

SEARCHING FOR SPRING by Patricia A. Murphy. 224 pp.
Novel about the recovery of love.   ISBN 0-941483-00-2   8.95

DUSTY'S QUEEN OF HEARTS DINER by Lee Lynch. 240 pp.
Romantic blue-collar novel.   ISBN 0-941483-01-0   8.95

PARENTS MATTER by Ann Muller. 240 pp. Parents'
relationships with Lesbian daughters and gay sons.
                                           ISBN 0-930044-91-6   9.95

THE PEARLS by Shelley Smith. 176 pp. Passion and fun in
the Caribbean sun. ISBN 0-930044-93-2　　7.95

MAGDALENA by Sarah Aldridge. 352 pp. Epic Lesbian novel
set on three continents. ISBN 0-930044-99-1　　8.95

THE BLACK AND WHITE OF IT by Ann Allen Shockley.
144 pp. Short stories. ISBN 0-930044-96-7　　7.95

SAY JESUS AND COME TO ME by Ann Allen Shockley. 288
pp. Contemporary romance. ISBN 0-930044-98-3　　8.95

LOVING HER by Ann Allen Shockley. 192 pp. Romantic love
story. ISBN 0-930044-97-5　　7.95

MURDER AT THE NIGHTWOOD BAR by Katherine V.
Forrest. 240 pp. A Kate Delafield mystery. Second in a series.
ISBN 0-930044-92-4　　8.95

ZOE'S BOOK by Gail Pass. 224 pp. Passionate, obsessive love
story. ISBN 0-930044-95-9　　7.95

WINGED DANCER by Camarin Grae. 228 pp. Erotic Lesbian
adventure story. ISBN 0-930044-88-6　　8.95

PAZ by Camarin Grae. 336 pp. Romantic Lesbian adventurer
with the power to change the world. ISBN 0-930044-89-4　　8.95

SOUL SNATCHER by Camarin Grae. 224 pp. A puzzle, an
adventure, a mystery — Lesbian romance. ISBN 0-930044-90-8　　8.95

THE LOVE OF GOOD WOMEN by Isabel Miller. 224 pp.
Long-awaited new novel by the author of the beloved *Patience
and Sarah*. ISBN 0-930044-81-9　　8.95

THE HOUSE AT PELHAM FALLS by Brenda Weathers. 240
pp. Suspenseful Lesbian ghost story. ISBN 0-930044-79-7　　7.95

HOME IN YOUR HANDS by Lee Lynch. 240 pp. More stories
from the author of *Old Dyke Tales*. ISBN 0-930044-80-0　　7.95

EACH HAND A MAP by Anita Skeen. 112 pp. Real-life poems
that touch us all. ISBN 0-930044-82-7　　6.95

SURPLUS by Sylvia Stevenson. 342 pp. A classic early Lesbian
novel. ISBN 0-930044-78-9　　7.95

PEMBROKE PARK by Michelle Martin. 256 pp. Derring-do
and daring romance in Regency England. ISBN 0-930044-77-0　　7.95

THE LONG TRAIL by Penny Hayes. 248 pp. Vivid adventures
of two women in love in the old west. ISBN 0-930044-76-2　　8.95

HORIZON OF THE HEART by Shelley Smith. 192 pp. Hot
romance in summertime New England. ISBN 0-930044-75-4　　7.95

AN EMERGENCE OF GREEN by Katherine V. Forrest. 288
pp. Powerful novel of sexual discovery. ISBN 0-930044-69-X　　9.95

THE LESBIAN PERIODICALS INDEX edited by Claire
Potter. 432 pp. Author & subject index. ISBN 0-930044-74-6　　29.95

DESERT OF THE HEART by Jane Rule. 224 pp. A classic;
basis for the movie *Desert Hearts*. ISBN 0-930044-73-8   8.95

SPRING FORWARD/FALL BACK by Sheila Ortiz Taylor.
288 pp. Literary novel of timeless love. ISBN 0-930044-70-3   7.95

FOR KEEPS by Elisabeth Nonas. 144 pp. Contemporary novel
about losing and finding love. ISBN 0-930044-71-1   7.95

TORCHLIGHT TO VALHALLA by Gale Wilhelm. 128 pp.
Classic novel by a great Lesbian writer. ISBN 0-930044-68-1   7.95

LESBIAN NUNS: BREAKING SILENCE edited by Rosemary
Curb and Nancy Manahan. 432 pp. Unprecedented autobiographies
of religious life. ISBN 0-930044-62-2   9.95

THE SWASHBUCKLER by Lee Lynch. 288 pp. Colorful novel
set in Greenwich Village in the sixties. ISBN 0-930044-66-5   8.95

MISFORTUNE'S FRIEND by Sarah Aldridge. 320 pp. Historical Lesbian novel set on two continents. ISBN 0-930044-67-3   7.95

A STUDIO OF ONE'S OWN by Ann Stokes. Edited by
Dolores Klaich. 128 pp. Autobiography. ISBN 0-930044-64-9   7.95

SEX VARIANT WOMEN IN LITERATURE by Jeannette
Howard Foster. 448 pp. Literary history. ISBN 0-930044-65-7   8.95

A HOT-EYED MODERATE by Jane Rule. 252 pp. Hard-hitting
essays on gay life; writing; art. ISBN 0-930044-57-6   7.95

INLAND PASSAGE AND OTHER STORIES by Jane Rule.
288 pp. Wide-ranging new collection. ISBN 0-930044-56-8   7.95

WE TOO ARE DRIFTING by Gale Wilhelm. 128 pp. Timeless
Lesbian novel, a masterpiece. ISBN 0-930044-61-4   6.95

AMATEUR CITY by Katherine V. Forrest. 224 pp. A Kate
Delafield mystery. First in a series. ISBN 0-930044-55-X   8.95

THE SOPHIE HOROWITZ STORY by Sarah Schulman. 176
pp. Engaging novel of madcap intrigue. ISBN 0-930044-54-1   7.95

THE BURNTON WIDOWS by Vickie P. McConnell. 272 pp. A
Nyla Wade mystery, second in the series. ISBN 0-930044-52-5   7.95

OLD DYKE TALES by Lee Lynch. 224 pp. Extraordinary
stories of our diverse Lesbian lives. ISBN 0-930044-51-7   8.95

DAUGHTERS OF A CORAL DAWN by Katherine V. Forrest.
240 pp. Novel set in a Lesbian new world. ISBN 0-930044-50-9   8.95

AGAINST THE SEASON by Jane Rule. 224 pp. Luminous,
complex novel of interrelationships. ISBN 0-930044-48-7   8.95

LOVERS IN THE PRESENT AFTERNOON by Kathleen
Fleming. 288 pp. A novel about recovery and growth.
ISBN 0-930044-46-0   8.95

TOOTHPICK HOUSE by Lee Lynch. 264 pp. Love between
two Lesbians of different classes.   ISBN 0-930044-45-2   7.95

MADAME AURORA by Sarah Aldridge. 256 pp. Historical
novel featuring a charismatic "seer."   ISBN 0-930044-44-4   7.95

CURIOUS WINE by Katherine V. Forrest. 176 pp. Passionate
Lesbian love story, a best-seller.   ISBN 0-930044-43-6   8.95

BLACK LESBIAN IN WHITE AMERICA by Anita Cornwell.
141 pp. Stories, essays, autobiography.   ISBN 0-930044-41-X   7.95

CONTRACT WITH THE WORLD by Jane Rule. 340 pp.
Powerful, panoramic novel of gay life.   ISBN 0-930044-28-2   9.95

MRS. PORTER'S LETTER by Vicki P. McConnell. 224 pp.
The first Nyla Wade mystery.   ISBN 0-930044-29-0   7.95

TO THE CLEVELAND STATION by Carol Anne Douglas.
192 pp. Interracial Lesbian love story.   ISBN 0-930044-27-4   6.95

THE NESTING PLACE by Sarah Aldridge. 224 pp. A
three-woman triangle — love conquers all!   ISBN 0-930044-26-6   7.95

THIS IS NOT FOR YOU by Jane Rule. 284 pp. A letter to a
beloved is also an intricate novel.   ISBN 0-930044-25-8   8.95

FAULTLINE by Sheila Ortiz Taylor. 140 pp. Warm, funny,
literate story of a startling family.   ISBN 0-930044-24-X   6.95

ANNA'S COUNTRY by Elizabeth Lang. 208 pp. A woman
finds her Lesbian identity.   ISBN 0-930044-19-3   8.95

PRISM by Valerie Taylor. 158 pp. A love affair between two
women in their sixties.   ISBN 0-930044-18-5   6.95

THE MARQUISE AND THE NOVICE by Victoria Ramstetter.
108 pp. A Lesbian Gothic novel.   ISBN 0-930044-16-9   6.95

OUTLANDER by Jane Rule. 207 pp. Short stories and essays
by one of our finest writers.   ISBN 0-930044-17-7   8.95

ALL TRUE LOVERS by Sarah Aldridge. 292 pp. Romantic
novel set in the 1930s and 1940s.   ISBN 0-930044-10-X   8.95

A WOMAN APPEARED TO ME by Renee Vivien. 65 pp. A
classic; translated by Jeannette H. Foster. ISBN 0-930044-06-1   5.00

CYTHEREA'S BREATH by Sarah Aldridge. 240 pp. Romantic
novel about women's entrance into medicine.
                                            ISBN 0-930044-02-9   6.95

TOTTIE by Sarah Aldridge. 181 pp. Lesbian romance in the
turmoil of the sixties.   ISBN 0-930044-01-0   6.95

THE LATECOMER by Sarah Aldridge. 107 pp. A delicate love
story.   ISBN 0-930044-00-2   6.95

ODD GIRL OUT by Ann Bannon.   ISBN 0-930044-83-5   5.95
I AM A WOMAN 84-3; WOMEN IN THE SHADOWS 85-1;   each
JOURNEY TO A WOMAN 86-X; BEEBO BRINKER 87-8. Golden
oldies about life in Greenwich Village.

JOURNEY TO FULFILLMENT, A WORLD WITHOUT MEN, and   3.95
RETURN TO LESBOS. All by Valerie Taylor   each

These are just a few of the many Naiad Press titles — we are the oldest and
largest lesbian/feminist publishing company in the world. Please request a
complete catalog. We offer personal service; we encourage and welcome direct
mail orders from individuals who have limited access to bookstores carrying
our publications.